ASSEGAI!

ASSEGAI!

Nickie McMenemy

Saturday Review Press

NEW YORK

AUTHOR'S NOTE

Assegai! is based on the life of Tshaka, King of the Zulus, as recorded in the diaries of Henry Francis Fynn.

The historical characters in the novel include:
    John Cane
    Dingane
    Dingiswayo
    Henry Francis Fynn
    Jacob (Hlambamanzi)
    Lieut. King
    Mhlangana
    Nandi
    Ngwadi
    Sigujana
    Tshaka Zulu
    Umbopha and his sister
Thola is a purely fictional character.

ASSEGAI!

1

BECAUSE of her beauty she did not die when the rotting timber in the slaver collapsed: some altercation between the captain and the new part-owner of the ship took place and she was brought out from the darkness below deck; angry hands ripped away all that covered her and the two men argued furiously concerning her merits and the probable price she would fetch.

When the invading water swelled in green, translucent billows over the ship she was engulfed in the surging swiftness and carried beyond the breakers towards the shore; half blind, her mind already straying into the dim regions of unconsciousness, she nevertheless reacted instantly to the feel of solid ground beneath her and scrabbled drunkenly through the small, curling waves onto the hot sand. Here instinct again motivated her almost mindless body; she raised herself into a crouching position and in great heaves rejected the poison of the salt water she had swallowed; afterwards she sank back on the burning sand, vaguely surprised that she was now being plunged into darkness when, a moment before, she had been exposed to a glaring intensity of scorching sunlight. More and more her consciousness receded; her blistering lips opened slackly and her bruised limbs relaxed; presently she lay so still that her body, viewed from the slopes of the rising coastline, resembled a dark mound of driftwood carelessly tossed by the incoming tide upon the golden sands.

The men, when they ventured down from the hills, did not know what to make of her. They approached with great caution, grouping around her, but keeping a safe distance. When she stirred they retreated and exclamations of fear burst from them.

Waveringly the girl levered herself onto her knees and gradually the blurred outlines of moving figures coalesced into solid shapes: lean men, naked except for loincloths of animal skins; one man had a plume of white feathers on his head and when he turned his neck sharply towards her, the tall plumes threw faint shadows on the black sheen of his skin.

She tried to speak and, at last, succeeded; her words were greeted by staccato clicks and the resonance of flowing, vowel-ending vocables.

They seemed so strong, these black men; and, despite their obvious fear, they were so threatening in their attitudes that she, who had not wept since she was a child, lost the chains of self-control which slavery had forged for her and howled in her terror.

The men drew apart and appeared to hold a hurried consultation; her utter weakness forced the sobs to catch in her throat and dwindle to nothingness, and she thought she caught a familiar word. 'UBaba,' one man seemed to say to the huge black with the plumed headdress, 'Ubaba.'

'I do not know how old I am,' she called out desperately, riven with the need to establish contact, 'but I am not a child.'

Suddenly she became aware of her complete nakedness and crouched on her knees and crossed her arms over her chest. Again the men withdrew and their rough voices cut through the little distance which separated them from her; faintness subdued her and affected the harsh monotone of mingling sounds so that hoarse whispers struck her ears as monstrous outcries.

She had never before experienced such fear. Her life, she knew, had been fairly sheltered: she had been born into slavery; had lived with her ebony-skinned mother for a brief six years; her father, whose mixed blood had imparted to her her copper-brown colour and pliant hair, she had not known at all. The desolation she had felt the day she was taken from her mother and sold was in no way comparable to her present wretchedness; there had been a finality in that separation that had produced in her an instinctive surrendering to her fate. The crippled woman who had purchased her had possessed wit and intelligence, but neither beauty nor gentleness; and had required not so much a servant as a servile companion. The slave girl, quiet and malleable, had been taught to read and write; to embroider and to assist at her mistress's toilette; she had learned to be a faithful reflection of her owner's moods. When her mistress died identity had somehow become almost non-existent; passively she had submitted to a second sale and purchase; afterwards, with animal fortitude, she had endured her transportation to the slaver and the hideousness of the voyage, a hideousness which had culminated in that moment when the green translucence of the towering waves had deluged the ship and swept her towards land.

Formerly she had possessed a confused awareness of what she feared: whippings, cruel owners, common calamities which others shared; now she was weaponless against the unknown and the unfamiliar.

A command came from the group of men; she had known authority all her life and now, despite her distress, recognised it by its intonation. As she looked up the brilliant sunlight pierced her eyes and made her blink in pain. His body poised as if in readiness for instant flight, a man came forward and put a tentative hand on her shoulder. She cringed away from him and he jerked her to her feet and beckoned for her to follow him; and she obeyed, her legs dragging because of her

3

weakness and extreme weariness; the rest of the company padded at her heels.

In this alien country, this unknown portion of Africa, midway, she supposed, between Cape Town and Delagoa Bay, there were no roads, not even a rising column of smoke in the glittering air to betoken settled habitation; apparently the wilderness was peopled by wild and half-naked savages. The turgidly green vegetation flourished with suffocating prolificacy and tangled her feet in a snarled matting; but when she was led farther inland the jungle-like growth gave way to high grass which swayed in the wind; and clumps of queer, stunted-looking trees began to break the contour-line of the rounded hills.

Once the man ahead of her stopped so precipitately that she almost fell over him; he remained in his motionless, rigid attitude, and she sank down behind him and heard herself panting like a dog. Additional torture had come to her for thirst was now parching her throat; she wondered, confusedly, whether fear had perhaps driven her mad. She had, after all, on several occasions witnessed madness among the slaves in the hold of the ship; tortured minds had easily disposed of suffering and privation and substituted cool flowing water in place of foul bilge.

Swiftly, suddenly, the spear the leader had been carrying flashed forward; the man uttered a high-pitched, triumphant shout and bounded on ahead. A small animal kicked its slender legs; blood welled up and flowed over its glossy skin; quietly, a few seconds later, it died.

Now the savages lengthened their easy, half-loping stride, and she stumbled along with them; when pain and weariness reached an intolerable pinnacle she saw the huts against the hill: clusters of bee-hive shapes encircled by a timber palisade. Blood from the animal which the leader carried had spattered over her; and had she been able to see herself she would have laughed in hysteria at the idea that she, with her raw and bleeding feet, distended nostrils, crazed eyes and bulbously swollen lips, would change the fate of the people dwelling in this southern tip of Africa.

At the entrance to the palisade she fell forward and could not will herself to move; hands plucked at her and dragged her into some shelter, a hut she thought, and while she pleaded hoarsely for water frightened black women gathered around her and stared at her bovinely.

How long she had lain delirious on a mat woven of grass, her feverish body covered by a blanket made of animal skins, she never discovered; but she had a dim recollection of being offered, at intervals, a liquid that tasted like sour milk, and also of pieces of half-raw meat, unsalted, being stuffed into her mouth; once she had awakened in stifling darkness and had groped around; the low entrance, which obviously could only be entered on hands and knees, had been securely blocked by a thick covering, probably a stopper made from woven grass.

Then, suddenly, the fever-mists rolled away from her mind, leaving it fresh and clear and, surprisingly, full of hope. The grass sleeping mat, the skin covering, the calabash of water, all subconsciously familiar, proved that care had at least been expended upon her: had her captors wished her dead, she decided, they would not have provided food and shelter.

When she was confident of her strength she crawled out of the hut into the blazing sunlight; several of the women stopped and stared at her – without friendliness or animosity. A little naked boy ran past, giggling; she remembered her own lack of clothing and hesitated, and then saw that a beaded fringe was suspended from a thong which encircled her waist. Her breasts were bare.

She smiled timidly at the women but received no response: then a very fat woman waddled towards her and addressed her commandingly; not understanding she shook her head, and the woman motioned to her to sit down near the entrance of the hut. Immediately she obeyed and each day that was the position allocated to her. Now and again she was visited by an old woman who was spectacularly clothed in skins and adorned with what seemed to be necklaces and bracelets of teeth and small bones. She could not hide her fear and this appeared to please the old woman.

Presently more freedom was permitted her, and she wandered about and watched the cattle being driven away by small herdboys: so few cattle, thin and lean. There were two bulls, one white, one black, and these were the scrawniest of all. She ventured after the women when they went to hoe patches of ground and was an interested spectator when they ground corn and brewed some sort of beverage.

Day by day she listened and observed and very gradually began to pick up a word here and a word there; and when she was led down to the river which flowed sluggishly between ochre-coloured banks she understood when she was ordered to wash herself.

She came to know Malanga. Often she had intercepted the covert stares this tall boy had sent her and, late one evening, the stifling heat forced her to venture out of her hut; all was utter quietness except for the low breathing near her; her eyes accustomed themselves to darkness and when the moon sailed out from behind the dense clouds she recognised Malanga. He vanished with the silence and swiftness of woodsmoke caught in a gust of wind, but the following night and the night after he returned; and in the end she began to exchange

6

a few halting words with him. And she discovered that Malanga was different from his people, as she was different: he had been born in a hut within the palisade yet, obscurely, he did not belong. One night, as if by common consent, they walked towards the entrance of the kraal and sat down in the shadow, darker than the dark night, cast by the palings at the back of which moonlight gleamed faintly.

'Umfo uyafika,' Malanga whispered to her, and she translated his words into her own language, 'Stranger, she arrives.' The statement did not seem to call for any comment and she waited in silence.

'Woman old she had child stranger,' Malanga continued.

Had the old, bone-bedecked woman truly adopted her? Reserve had become a prudent habit and she did not enquire.

'Stranger she comes from where?' Malanga asked.

Not knowing the word for 'sea' she shook her head, and then murmured, 'Water big.'

Malanga, who appeared to be in his late teens, made an awed sound, shivered and then rose quickly and slipped into the darker shadows; and she heard his muted footfalls as he padded into the hut reserved for the boys.

But he appeared to be powerless against the temptation to seek her out and again and again she found him waiting at the entrance to the palisade. Everyone else ignored her entirely; and it was through Malanga that she learned to string words together to form phrases and, eventually, whole sentences; the time came when she understood what was said to her without first having to translate each word into her own language.

'Truly you came from great water,' Malanga told her one night. 'My father was present when you were found on shore. Can you draw in breath under water?'

7

'No,' she replied, and even when he pressed her she refused to elaborate.

'You are fortunate to be alive. Ukhula is woman wise; she has been in hills and spoken with spirits and she has been under water in river where people-of-water-life taught her mysteries. She said you should live. You are black like people of ours but your hair is long. Your hair is smoother. You are now child of Ukhula. You like people of ours?'

'I like,' she said, and thought wanly of the extreme heat and the clouds of persistent flies, the unvarying diet and the dismal nights, the unrelieved monotony of existence. But the terrible heat provided the greatest test of endurance: no wonder that in Malanga's language one word, 'ilanga', signified 'day' as well as 'sun'.

'You have told no one your name,' Malanga continued. 'We have given you name,' and he waited slyly.

'What is my name?' she asked, bending forward.

'Thola,' he told her and smiled.

'To – hola?'

'Thola,' Malanga repeated.

'Because I was found, I suppose. It means "to find", doesn't it? I have not told you my name because you could not say it. You have no letter in your language to make the sound of it.'

'What is "letter"?' His tongue stumbled over the foreign word.

'Consonants and vowels,' she said, speaking in her own language, 'have symbols to convey their sounds. But you have no written language. And it does not seem as if there is an "r" in your language.'

Startled, Malanga jumped to his feet and she soothed him, smiling into the moonlight, and murmured, 'Do not be afraid. I was only speaking my own language, but I cannot tell you what I was saying for you have no

8

words to match my words. We will speak of other things.'

The following day men from a neighbouring kraal arrived and held long discussions with the headman; a special beast was slaughtered for the strangers and a good deal of merrymaking and drinking disturbed the usual routine. Late that night Thola found Malanga in the customary place and greeted him gently; she seated herself and the soft sound of the wind rustling in the tall grass whispered towards her.

'You look sad,' she observed. 'All the others laughed when they danced.'

'Hlalisa is soon to be married,' the boy sighed. 'I am not circumcised. I can do nothing.'

Questioningly Thola repeated the strange word and Malanga explained.

'No one is man until he is circumcised. Only men can marry. First I must ask my father to let me be circumcised. Then I must wait for full-grown moon. But if harvest is bad – if rain is slow in coming – I must wait again.'

'Does Hlalisa wish to marry you?'

'She would like to come into my hut – when I have one – but many cattle have been offered for her and she is proud of such large dowry. I am full of sorrow,' he added simply.

'Perhaps your father would hurry with the circumcision if you spoke to him?' She had attempted too involved a sentence and had to repeat herself several times before the boy grasped her meaning.

'My father would not,' Malanga said; he seemed to withdraw into the darkness; and then, in the softest of whispers, he explained. 'I will tell you what I would not tell anyone else. You speak so little. I am afraid to be circumcised.'

Ironic laughter bubbled in her throat: she, the

9

sophisticate, whose mistress had, in her youth, corres-
ponded with Rousseau, was having firsthand experience
of savage simplicity.

'I suppose everyone in your age group is afraid,' she
comforted.

'They do not say so. They boast.' Gloomily Malanga
rested his head upon his hands. 'I should not speak of
this: blade of spear is sharp but brings much pain.' He
rose to his feet in one quick, lithe movement. 'Tomorrow you will see much. Keep to yourself.'

Thola watched the darkness of night accept and
swallow the boy; then she made her way quietly to her
own hut. The intense heat oppressed her again but she
did not dare leave the entrance open: marauding
animals sometimes ventured within the palisade.

If she had a light to dispel the cloying darkness, if she
had a book to read, she thought, life would be less in-
supportable; the promise of a future of intolerable bore-
dom carried with it a ragged percipience of ultimate
insanity. She was lost amongst savages whose music
consisted of a wild, elementary chanting; whose un-
restrained dancing was indicative of unpleasant sexual
gestures; she had discovered noble simplicity in its
starkest form. God give that her former mistress could
somehow be brought back to life and then precipitated
into the simplicity she had so much admired: if that
cripple were indeed blazing in God's hellfire, she was
still not being subjected to the intensity of torture her
slave was suffering.

Thola moved restlessly upon her hard sleeping mat
and reflected that the mat was spread upon a floor made
of cow-dung: one could not get nearer to nature than
that. The excitement Malanga had offered for the
following day would probably turn out to be an event so
fatuous that it would only increase her sense of deadly
ennui. Malanga's people were too predictable; they

were endlessly preoccupied with the basic necessities of life; laws only existed because they were conducive to tribal survival; abstract justice held no meaning whatsoever; in everything the community mattered, not the individual.

The wooden block which served as a pillow made her neck ache and she pushed it away and dropped her head on her arms and wept despairingly. She had not even achieved freedom: she was still a captive.

Insidiously the passage of time lent a false value to the years she had spent with her crippled mistress: a mellow light dissipated the shadows and the cripple was revealed as a benefactress, an owner not too unkind; almost Thola cried for her in nostalgic longing. Then reason took command and brought its own revelation, and memory recalled half-forgotten cruelties: the incisiveness of barbed words, the indignity of unexpected and unearned blows, the ridicule and contempt so often endured.

As now, she had never had any decisive voice in her own life; not as a child; not as a woman. Every hour of her day and night had been regulated by another's whim; every action circumscribed; every morsel of food, every stitch of clothing had depended on the cripple's choice.

But at least her life had not hung in balance; not obviously so. Malanga's people held even the power of death in their savage hands.

Here was true desolation.

2

EARLY in the morning there was a great stir in the
kraal and Thola, remembering Malanga's advice,
crouched in her hut. But the commotion, the atmosphere of suspense, excited her and she dragged her
sleeping-mat to the entrance and lay down, curling her
body to the rounded contours of the hut walls. From
that position, herself unseen, she peered out.

The black bull, that scrawny beast, had been led out
of the cattle-shed and it was bellowing in terror, as if
anticipating some frightful ordeal; the ragged echoes of
its roaring invaded the valleys where the mist hung low,
and recoiled hollowly from the boulder-strewn hillsides.

A woman moaned and whimpered and moved restlessly. Thola recognised her: a few days previously this
woman had stammeringly described a dream to a group
of attentive listeners. In her dream she had had a snake
lustfully dwelling within her, near her uterus. Afterwards, when the woman had trudged down to the river,
one of the Chief's minor wives had observed scathingly,
'It is not dream. Possessed is she by inyoka: snake.
When snake comes to live in woman's body, always
woman speaks of dream.'

Now a swelling murmur of animal fear issued from
the central cattle-shed and increased the tide of panic
already heaving so urgently in the bull. The mist
gathered over the kraal and rolled over the people and
many hands, seemingly disembodied members of in-
substantial bodies, emerged and pushed the bull and
brought its bulk crashing to the ground; skilfully,

swiftly, mist-shrouded hands, wielding sharp instruments, slashed at leg tendons. As if blanketed in a numbing cloud of horror, all sound ceased; even the cattle fell silent. Then the bull, as it was forced upright, roared again in terrible agony; sharp sticks prodded into its quivering hide, piercing the thick skin and drawing blood; and shudderingly the bull limped forward, wanly seeking to escape its tormentors, unable to do more than to draw deep, sighing breaths. Thola experienced an empathic anguish: it was as if the pain would endure for ever. The sticks whipped with greater venom and the hobbling pace quickened; and all the world reeled into a red madness of hurt and fear. One man, the head of the kraal, padded at the bull's side, made an incision in the animal, and inserted a predatory hand into the cavity and grasped the huge heart and pressed and constricted it. The bull gasped and died.

Thola, her hands trembling and fumbling so much that hours seemed to pass before she accomplished the easy little task, closed the entrance to her hut, and lay down again on her mat and tried to shut her ears against the feasting and the jesting that followed. Her complacent acceptance of simple savagery had vanished: here was neither childishness nor gentleness. She was overwhelmed by an urgent desire to escape: even the brutality she had suffered in the hold of the slaver had not been enough to condition her to the ceremony she had witnessed.

It required real courage for her to steal out of her hut at nightfall to meet Malanga, but now she was driven by an obsessive need to understand her position; for the first time she felt an urgent necessity to question and receive answers.

Malanga was preoccupied with his own affairs. 'Moon will now start being eaten up,' he told her, anxiously peering at her. 'Then moon will grow again and be reborn.'

'The bull . . .' she began, and fell silent, horror returning to her.

'Sacrifice for rain. So is sacrifice of my living flesh for manhood. Moon will grow again and again but one cannot be circumcised again and again. I sat in my father's presence and asked for circumcision. If rainfall is good, circumcision will be done,' and he trembled a little.

Unwillingly Thola focused her attention on him; she did not really believe that he was a coward: he was too tall and lithe, his small head set on a sturdy, muscle-rippling neck. He was, she decided, a misfit: he was sensitive.

'I am son of Chief,' Malanga continued. 'First blade of spear will be used on another who will receive all that is hurtful upon it. Cleansed by that other's blood, blade will then be used on me.'

'Do you – your tribe – do you eat *people*?' Thola asked, the words spurting out, and sickness came to the pit of her stomach.

The boy looked at her enquiringly, almost as if her question puzzled him.

'I have heard that sometimes people are placed in the cooking-pot and eaten,' she added, and waited.

'Hau! That we do not,' Malanga replied, after a moment's silence. 'Some eat human flesh because of hunger – but not here. We use flesh of man and woman and bones – sometimes – to make magic medicine, and a chief may eat to get strength and power. It is said that in land of AmaZulu much medicine is made. That is land of great Zulu king. Tshaka.'

Tshaka. Afterwards she decided that fate, after all, ruled one's destiny. The name held a magic of its own; her blood suddenly coursed warmly, as if turned into a surging river; and over and over her heartbeats drummed out the syllables of the great king's name. She found difficulty in moving her tongue to speak. 'Are your people not of the AmaZulu?'

'It is hard to say,' Malanga answered her. 'We are what is left of tribe who fled from him. World fears Tshaka.'

'What is the meaning of "AmaZulu"?'

'People of heaven. Zulu.' He made of the 'z' a hard sound, and drew out the 'u' into a long, powerful vowel-resonance. 'Tshaka has mighty army and strongest and greatest warriors. They are without fear.'

She caught the lingering envy in his voice and later the recollection of his grudging desire aided her.

'Soon,' Malanga continued, 'you too will undergo initiation rite; then you will truly become witch's daughter.'

'What will be done to me?'

'It is secret,' he said, and laughed. 'You will be alone in hut and all hair from your body will be taken away, except hair of your head. You are beautiful, though thin, people say. Witch will be given many cattle for your bride price. Much lobola.' The boy laughed unexpectedly, a high-pitched cackle which characterised all the men's laughter, even though they mostly possessed low, bass voices. 'I cannot have Hlalisa. Perhaps I will take you into my hut. If my father gives lobola cattle for you, you will always be my most important wife. We will take you as one of us,' and again Malanga laughed. 'We thought at first you were some animal come out of sea; yet you had head and two arms and feet, but skin of you was like ours mixed with yellow, and colour of red-brown sand on river-bank contained in your eyes, and your hair grows and hangs upon your shoulders. Although it is not smooth like hair of animal, but half smooth and half like ours.'

15

'I do not want to marry,' she said and she, who was always so still, moved fretfully.

'Then you must go to Tshaka,' Malanga murmured, a sly edge to his voice. 'Great king does not marry. In his isigodlo he has only sisters whom he does not deflower.' He was overcome with mirth at the thought of Thola's living in Tshaka's harem.

'Tshaka lives a life of chastity then,' Thola murmured, vaguely surprised.

'Hau! He does not. You do not know of way delight comes without harm. It is true you come out of sea and know nothing.'

'Tell me.'

'I should not even be speaking with you like this,' Malanga objected, 'it is not my place to tell you of customs which only mothers tell their daughters.'

'I have no mother,' Thola whispered hopefully.

'Witch is your mother.'

'I am afraid of her.'

That he readily understood. 'To deflower woman is great offence,' Malanga said at last, just when it seemed he would refuse to explain. 'A man may take a woman – a maiden – to sleep under same blanket with him. Two such ones will know what it is to love, but maiden will not be harmed. But with Tshaka you will never know; he has countless maidens in his isigodlo.'

Thola sat in silence, greatly puzzled; then, suddenly, she remembered a discussion her former mistress had once held with an eminent intellectual; almost, as if the years had rolled back, she heard the sly, malicious voice disparaging the farcical practice of agape among the early Christians. Abruptly she left Malanga and returned to her hut; and, fantastically, she was enslaved again; the walls of the hut receded and she was humbly seated at the feet of the sophisticated cripple behind whose elaborately coiffured head gleamed wine-coloured, heavy velvet curtains; soft light from the tall, wax candles, arrogant in their silver candlesticks, flickered on diamond earrings, and each turn of the scraggy neck caused the earrings to sway in little arcs of subdued scintillation. Outside a dog barked and the vivid picture dissolved and reality swooped back. What disgust that evil woman would have expressed at the method of companionship Malanga had just revealed; yet Thola, in herself, experienced no revulsion. Almost imperceptibly she was adapting herself to the savage way of life and accepting a culture that was or should have been alien; but, in this untamed country with its seething heat, so much seemed natural and right, and she began to understand the origin of the muted footfalls she had often heard late at night. With the coming of darkness the men, women and children had always withdrawn into the huts; the doorways had been securely closed and fires lighted so that thick smoke swirled around and up towards the small openings in the roofs of the huts; people had sprawled in sleep with a blanket of smoke weaving a few inches above their heads; they were so accustomed to the bitter woodsmoke fumes that few coughed or noticed the stinging of eyes. At first the silence had been disturbed only by the animals in their kraals; then, secretively, slowly, the footfalls had come: young men and women, she now realised, stealing out of their huts to meet in the darkness beyond the kraal where the grass grew thickly and sheltered them from all who would trespass on their privacy.

Thola relaxed on her sleeping-mat; perhaps even now Malanga was leading Hlalisa away to the secrecy of some trysting place . . .

Hlalisa waited passively but Malanga did not draw her into the warmth beneath his skin covering; once

17

Malanga shivered violently and Hlalisa muttered that it was cold but Malanga returned no assenting murmur. He was not cold: he was afraid. The roaring agony of the bull bellowed in his ears and he shuddered away from the thought of the pain the circumcision rites would bring to him.

'When I become a man,' Malanga said at last, 'in whose hut will you please a husband?'

The girl shrugged lightly. 'I have heard my mother speak. Soon the man who wants me will catch me when I am alone and take me to his kraal. What can I do?'

'You must be careful not to be alone,' he sighed. 'Let us return to our huts,' he wanted to say, 'I am weary. Let us sleep then we will not be afraid,' but he said none of these things because Hlalisa would not understand. Suddenly he recoiled with horror at the thought that he might be bewitched: witchcraft might have induced the great fear in him. Perhaps the man who wanted Hlalisa had arranged with one of the amaxhwele, the witchdoctors into whose tribe his own people had merged when they fled from Tshaka, to have a spell laid upon him. Perhaps the sorcerer had already made him accursed with cowardice so that at the circumcision rite he, Malanga, would show abject terror: he would be expelled; he would be refused initiation; he would have to wait for a year, perhaps longer, before qualifying for circumcision again.

Somewhere in the long grass a girl laughed shrilly and a male voice growled a warning. Malanga sighed and reluctantly drew Hlalisa to him, and she came instantly. She had no fear: Malanga knew well enough that girls were regularly examined and that he would incur severe penalties if he broke the tribal law. And Hlalisa had been warned of cases where maidens had conceived and she was careful, despite her acquiescence.

Afterwards Malanga was surly with her and they

walked back to the huts in silence, gliding like stealthy shadows through the long grass; now and again they whispered reassuringly to the native dogs, thin skulking forms, always hungry. A low moaning sigh came from the cattle and, without a word, Hlalisa turned away from Malanga and crept into the girls' hut and lay down and fell asleep within seconds.

And Malanga entered the boys' hut and also tried to sleep: Malanga who was not-yet-man. . . .

And in another hut lay Nontaka, shudderingly afraid, yet her fear was faintly tinged with triumph. Inyoka, the snake, moved sluggishly within her and she repressed a cry. Her inyoka was not evil: he was good and harmless; yet he was a snake and could bite and would defend himself. Sometimes she was afraid that he would refuse to leave when she requested him to vacate her body. He was powerful but he could not give her children. He might inflict a wound and then there might never be little ones. Ukhula, the witch, also was possessed by a snake, a wicked one that, but he had given her a daughter: a maiden from the sea.

'Bird will give you eggs from her nest,' she whispered softly to the snake. 'I who am called Nontaka, which means bird, will give you eggs.' Faintly she heard the charmed river-people calling her.

Some distance away from the kraal the moonswept river sobbed and purled where its gleaming water gushed over rocks into a miniature waterfall. In the river lived the half-fish people; like Ukhula's daughter who had come from the mysteries of the sea, they had long hair and smooth, brown skins. Sometimes these people wanted a sacrifice and then they called: a beast might plunge into the river, a man or a woman; even a child. If anyone wept for the sacrifice, he or she would be gone forever.

Insistently the people of the river called to Nontaka, but sleep stopped her from running to them and leaping into the water where their long hair swayed in the moving stream and their voices sang to the accompaniment of the swishing lullaby of the river. . . .

The following day the three strangers arrived at the kraal. As usual the morning was hot. A solitary bird skimmed overhead, the sun glinting sharply on its white wings, and its shadow darted and swooped across the red, sun-scorched earth. At the far end of the kraal women busied themselves around vast black cooking-pots and the acrid woodsmoke drifted above them and swirled outwards and filled the air with burning bitterness. They sang together as they worked: three notes in a minor key, and the refrain was now and again eclipsed by a repetitive, pit-a-pat-sounding imitative call. The women sang:

> 'Falls rain sweet,
> Rain sweet,
> Bi! Bi! Bi!'

the initial consonant in the repetitive phrase violently implosive. The sad, nostalgically lovely sounds whispered away in the wind.

The strangers crouched on their haunches some distance away and waited to be approached and presently a young man went to enquire their business and brought then into the kraal; they sat respectfully in the Chief's presence and the Chief ordered an ox, which he could ill spare, to be slaughtered for them and a hut was allocated to them. They were spies, newly returned from the borders or Tshaka's country, which lay hidden to the east, and their stomachs were distended with news of Tshaka of the AmaZulu.

'Ewe!' the Chief rumbled heavily as they related terrible stories – how a baby impaled on a stake at the

20

entrance of a kraal proclaimed its total devastation by Zulu warriors.

'Tshaka,' one stranger said, spitting out the name, and the syllables lingered and possessed magic and sent heated blood coursing through sluggish arteries.

Thola strained her ears: she could not go close to the old Chief; she was an intruder and, in any case, his daughters-in-law were with her, and he was taboo to them. All the women kept their eyes carefully averted.

'He is an upstart,' the old Chief complained. 'What has happened to the ones who held their spears against him?'

'Tshaka ate them up,' a stranger replied simply. 'The uncircumcised elephant stamped them beneath his feet.'

'He is not even a man,' the Chief grumbled.

'That is so. He is uncircumcised,' a stranger agreed. 'Nevertheless, all eat the earth before him.' Death after all, fell swiftly upon those who opposed Tshaka. 'None of his warriors may marry until he gives the word and a man cannot marry until he has been circumcised. Wives come to his warriors towards the sunset of their lives.'

'It has been said,' one of the man's companions added, 'that he has done away with circumcision. When his mother conceived, his father was uncircumcised.'

'How so?' asked the Chief, pretending to be greatly shocked. He knew all about Tshaka, of course, but endless discussion characterised conversation.

'Senzangakhona, chief of the AmaZulu, then a small tribe under the rule of Dingiswayo, broke the law and deflowered a woman called Nandi while he was still uncircumcised. When the child lived within her it was said that the cycle of the moon was without effect because of itShaka, the beetle that has such a restraining influence. The father of Tshaka could not order himself:

21

he hit at the snake in the pathway but instead of continuing straight on he burrowed into the home of the snake.'

'Yo!' chuckled the Chief, much amused by the graphic description, 'yo, yo, yo! Hear this, O young men, and do not do likewise, lest you bring more evil upon our land by giving life to another Tshaka.'

The strangers went on to describe Tshaka: their words ran together as if seeking to produce a paean of might, but words could not describe the king's awful power. Tshaka was a giant, an ogre, a monstrous man of great height and strength and power; a lion, an elephant, a leader and a ruler; certainly possessed of tremendous supernatural force.

Thola sat rigid under the enchantment laid upon her by the thought of this king, this extraordinary man.

'When Tshaka's regiments plant the soles of their feet upon the earth,' a stranger said, almost chanting, 'the earth gives off dust to hide them, and when they stamp their feet, as one man, the earth trembles beneath.' He rose and imitated a Zulu warrior's actions: he brought his right knee up and then let his foot thud down: 'Bayete!' he shouted, giving the Royal salute, 'bayete, Inkosi!'

Vividly Thola saw thousands of warriors saluting their king and, as if in a hallucination, for a moment dust obscured the sun and the earth shivered; and she heard the mighty rumble of male voices: 'Hail! Hail, Chief!'

When the strangers left events moved horribly and swiftly: Hlalisa went to the marriage ceremony, a general exodus following her, for all were intent on being present at the kraal over the hill where lived the man who had given lobola for the young girl. Hlalisa wept and protested against going but the man caught her and dragged her; and her wailing increased the farther she was dragged, her body bumping painfully over the rough ground. Thola had been ordered to remain in the kraal and through the days that followed she was aware of Nontaka's burning eyes, for the woman had also remained behind. Sometimes Thola was given a respite when Nontaka stumbled off to the hills, talking to some unseen companion, but most of the time she staggered around the kraal, always following Thola, the fever in her eyes glowing with a strange madness. In the quiet night, when the wind fell asleep, the singing from the marriage-kraal could be heard, so faint the rhythmic rise and fall of voices was scarcely audible; and this ghostly sound augmented Thola's awareness of danger.

The people returned, full of stories of the cattle slaughtered and eaten, and the beer imbibed, and the dancing and singing; and how the bride had screamed in the darkness of the hut and thus proved herself a maiden; and Malanga now had a dazed look about him, and a tightening of his mouth, as if pain gnawed at him; and Thola discovered that, according to custom, he and several other young men had slept in the bridal hut to be witnesses to the consummation of marriage. Hlalisa had fought against her husband and the man had called upon the witnesses to hold her down for him, and they had done so, for it was custom to do that when the bride was unwilling.

'Do men do thus in your land within the sea?' Malanga wanted to know from her.

'I do not know. I do not think so, ' she replied, and saw that the tears were running down his cheeks. 'If I could comfort you ...'

He turned away, staring beyond her towards the hills.

Later Malanga brought her news, so fearful, so full of the horror she had at first imagined and awaited: that horror which she had gradually learned to disregard as something that could not and would not happen.

Nontaka had been whispering that Thola was a witch: that she was a renegade who had left the river-people, the spirits of the river; had Thola not long hair and a skin light in colour? She had deserted the spirits and had tried to run away to the sea, but their witching power had followed her and had directed the men of the kraal to find her; she had been brought back but now she was an evil in the kraal, casting her spells upon its inmates. Soon the cattle would die; the women cease to bear; and the life-giving tears of heaven would dry up.

But that was not all. Nontaka was whispering that Malanga was bewitched as well. Malanga was inclined to believe that this was true.

'What happens,' Thola asked, 'if one is accused of being a witch?' In the dark she could just make out his form, but she knew that he was grey with fear.

'There is a smelling out,' Malanga told her and began to tremble. 'The wise ones point out the be-witched person. He can be killed at once, or he can be ordered to touch the blade of a spear which is white with heat – if his hand is not burnt, he is free. Or he can be given poison to drink. If he does not die, he is inno-cent.'

Thola crept closer to him, not to seek comfort – he was even more in fear than she was – but so as to be able to say very softly, 'Malanga, we must run away.'

A pause came in his breathing.

'We must run away,' she repeated urgently.

'Away?' he repeated stupidly. 'Where?'

'To Tshaka.'

Now it was out. Even if that magic name did not call him as it called her, the spur of fear would goad him into a decision to collaborate.

'I am not an animal out of the sea, Malanga, nor am I one of the river-people. I come from another land far across the great water. I am not a witch. Listen. I came in a house that floats on top of the water, the way a leaf floats upon the water of the river. The people in the countries beyond the great water travel in such houses from one country to another, across great oceans. The house in which I travelled was not well built and great waves struck it and broke it into little pieces, for the wood from which it was made had grown old and rotten, I think. I could not still the big swell in the sea; I could not bewitch the water.'

'You did not die in the water,' Malanga said, almost accusingly.

'The swell of the sea washed me onto the beach. You have seen how the river washes pieces of wood onto the dry sand.'

'That I have seen,' he concurred, his voice bewildered.

'We will be killed if we stay here,' she continued urgently. 'Let us run away to the land of Tshaka. There you do not even need to be circumcised. You can easily be a man in Tshaka's country.'

'Tshaka will surely eat us up.'

'If we stay here we will die in any case. Do you think that your hand can touch white hot metal and not burn? Has it ever happened that one accused of witchcraft passed that test unhurt?'

'It has not happened.'

'How is a witch killed? How will they kill us?'

Malanga shuddered. 'I will not say.'

'Let us rather be eaten by wild animals then – or killed by Tshaka. But I do not think we will die. We can walk along the line of the sea. We will find sweet water in the rivers and we can live on fish.'

'Fish may not be eaten,' Malanga interrupted.

'Blood of God!' Thola exclaimed impatiently; in her exasperation she had reverted to her own language and Malanga drew away from her. 'When you are starving you will eat anything, you fool. Malanga. Listen to me.

25

Let us gather together what food we can and let us go. It is early yet and by daybreak we can be far away.'

She could not determine how much influence she had over the boy. Fear settled in a cold chill upon her and then – and then – the desire to know Tshaka brought a flame, and a feverish warmth started to her cheeks. So strange, she thought, so strange. She had been conquered by a name.

'I cannot,' Malanga whispered, his teeth clicking together as he trembled.

'You can – or you will die. I will go by myself then, and leave you to be tortured and killed.'

He turned on her vindictively. 'You will not go. I will call loudly and people will run out and stop you.'

'Let us not quarrel,' she begged, trying to soothe him. 'Let us stand together for we have much to endure. Your spear will kill animals for food. You will be my protector.'

In the distance an owl hooted and in a hut a child began weeping over some babyish terror.

'Any moment it will be too late,' Thola warned. She had meant to frighten him and frightened herself. 'Nontaka might wake up . . .'

'She will not come out into the dark.'

'She will come out into the dark for she is the one who is bewitched. If the spirits tell her to come and accuse us she will do so. The white-hot blade of the spear will burn, Malanga. Think of the pain. Oh, think of the agony.'

But Malanga continued to make negatory sounds. It was as if some fatalistic acceptance had fallen over him; his fear-filled mind could not envisage escape. Quite suddenly Thola realised just how alien he was to her and she to him. Witchcraft was for him a real and vivid thing, an unquestioned manifestation. For her witchcraft was a possibility. She did not deny its existence;

some atavistic tendency in her blood responded to the thought of black magic and dark deeds; even the sophistication which had been imparted to her during her earlier years of slavery, even that allowed a burgeoning of the seeds of doubt. That evil woman who had owned her had never proved that witchcraft did not exist; sometimes, in fact, it had seemed as if the cripple had been possessed of some dreadful power.

Perhaps, Thola reasoned, during her years of servitude she had indeed been under her mistress's satanic influence; perhaps that was why her blood now leapt at the sound of Tshaka's name, he whom the natives clearly believed to be a kind of devil. She in herself had so little to counteract evil, not even much knowledge of religion. 'God,' her mistress used to cry, beating at her crippled limbs with frenzied hands, often when the fits of temper shook her, 'what God? Where? Who gave me these? And you straight limbs? There is no God!'

'Help me,' Thola prayed now, momentarily forgetting Malanga; childishly she folded her hands together and bent her head and her long hair fell forward on her shoulders; she spoke aloud in her own language. 'I do not know much about you. You know my mistress did not believe in you.' And, again childishly, she claimed protection: if she were His possession, He was also hers. 'Help me, *my* God,' she pleaded.

'Hau!' gasped Malanga, transfixed with terror.

'I have a spirit greater than the spirits of all your ancestors,' Thola told him passionately. 'He is a spirit that does only good. He makes the rain fall and the seeds grow and He saves those that are in danger. I have asked Him to help us and He will lead the way for us.'

The boy, gripping a pole in the palisade, levered himself up, as if his legs were too weak to respond to commands issued by his brain; and then, slowly, he backed away and a few seconds later she heard him

27

padding in the direction of the boys' hut. Thola, infinitely discouraged, crept to her own sleeping quarters and there, in the dark, she sat and waited.

At the first flush of dawn one of the Chief's daughters was gripped by phayiza. She began screaming in high-pitched, frantic tones that she was bewitched and burst out of her hut and ran around in circles, aimlessly; and the piercing, hysterical screaming increased in volume until it seemed as if her throat would rend itself through the intensity of her effort.

Thola edged out into the chill of the half-light; she was so afraid she could hardly breathe. Others had crawled out of their huts and people were milling around, some still half-asleep; their faces drawn and anxious they peered around; then Nontaka shouted, 'The witches. The witches have done this. They have brought – they have brought madness to the daughter of the Chief. Kill the witches! Kill the boy! He has become a witch with the sorceress who has long hair!'

Already Thola felt the agony of white-hot metal being pressed into her flesh; already she choked on bitter poison.

'Malanga!' she shouted, throwing her head back and letting her lungs explode in her calling, 'Malanga!' and, almost without knowing that she had formulated a plan, she began running. She was aware that someone was rushing after her, and did not have time to see if it was Malanga. Careless now of tribal law, she rushed into the Chief's hut and grabbed an assegai and then made for the cattle-shed, and saw that Malanga was indeed with her and that his eyes were bulging and his mouth hanging open in his great fear. The people disregarded the screaming girl and, from all sides, began to converge on Thola. 'Let the cattle go!' she shouted to Malanga; oh God, just when she needed such knowledge most, her unfamiliarity with the savage language confused her. 'Malanga! Chase the cattle out. Let them run over our – our pursuers. Hurry!' she sobbed, 'make them rush forward. Swiftly!' She turned and faced the maddened people and filled her lungs and screamed, 'Stand back. I call my spirit to scatter you. Be afraid. Be *full* of fear,' and then she swerved to one side as the cattle, lean and thin and tragically few, lumbered past her in utter confusion; and, grasping Malanga's hand, she began to run, out into the bareness surrounding the kraal, and then into the thick, high grass. Behind her clamoured deprecations and shouts of terror and, above all, the ululating of the hysterical girl. A spear sang past her head, and then another, and a sharp pain glanced along her left shoulder, and warm blood oozed down her back; but great strength came to her legs and heart and even when her breathing was hoarse and even when the boy running beside her began to fail she was still able to continue. When he suddenly fell flat into the long grass and she on top of him, even then, it seemed as if she could have continued running on and on.

'Malanga,' she called, but he was defeated in his fear and had flung an arm around his face and lay as if ready for death. 'We must not stay. Malanga!' and she shook him and was grateful for the high grass which hid them from sight. 'We must crawl away. Let us crawl away and around the kraal and your people will look for us here and go on looking for us in this direction and we will be gone. Oh, you who will never be a man, you are so craven coward, listen to me! Listen to me, and one day when you are a great warrior you will remember this moment and laugh at yourself. We do not need to die. We can live.'

'It is finished,' Malanga said at last, groaning; and suddenly, as if lightning had struck through the sky and lighted up a pathway upon the earth, hope flooded her in tremendous waves. The words spoken by the savage had a familiar ring; she had heard them before; surely she knew their origin. But it had not been finished: afterwards the great, the real glory had come.

'Look,' she said, 'I have been wounded. I have another plan. I will lead the people down to the river by letting my blood fall upon the grass and they will follow the trail and think we have gone into the river. They will cease looking for us. Come, let us crawl towards the river as quickly as possible. Blood can be left upon the banks and we will creep along the river and away to the sea and follow the line of the shore to some safe place.'

Malanga would not move and the sound of pursuit was becoming louder; she pressed the point of the assegai into his back and, although she was aware she could never carry out her threat, she said, with great determination, 'Move at once or I will kill you. I will kill you slowly.' Just when she felt that death would, after all, be inevitable, the boy moved shudderingly. On hands and feet, the assegai impeding them, they crawled down towards the river. She could not discard the only weapon they had: she remembered how, the day she had been found, one of her captors had killed an animal. Somehow, as they fled, Malanga would have to kill for food too. Now she was grateful for the injury she had received and glad that the wound was bleeding freely. She thought that a hesitant note had crept into the furious, bestial sounds of pursuit, and then she heard the bellow of the bull and, accompanying it, Nontaka's frenzied shrieking; and the falsetto sounds of the herd-boys lifting up their voices; and the bass ring of the men's comminations; and the hideous, menacing acuteness of the women's screaming. At the river's edge she paused to smear a handful of grass red with blood and she let the crimsoned greenness fall upon the bank; and then, pressing a fresh handful of grass to her shoulder to staunch the blood and using her right hand to support her body and also retain the spear, she forced Malanga to turn and crawl down towards the sea. Weakness numbed her limbs and she wondered that her body could hold so much blood; it was as if her strength now lay in the reddened path which was leading the trackers towards the river bank. When blackness started shutting out the sight of the world from her eyes, she paused and sank down, commanding Malanga to remain still, and the high grass seemed to close over her and over him and the burn in her lungs was like the burn her flesh would have suffered under white-hot metal. She could not speak for a long time and the boy, shivering and sighing, waited passively at her side; she did not think he was wholly conscious, or if he were, certainly his mind was not functioning properly: he was just a body that obeyed her orders, an animal submissive to her voice. She rested, almost supine on the ground, while the sounds of the hunt changed to expressions of incredulity and then stark fear; and she thought she heard rapid footfalls growing fainter, as if the people were running back to the kraal, away from the river. When, in her faintness, she released the pressure of her left hand upon her shoulder, no further blood spurted out, and she saw that the ragged edges of the wound were becoming black with congealed blood. She took another handful of grass and then plucked several long stems and shook Malanga and commanded, 'Plait the stems together and tie the grass-rope around my arm over this grass.'

Reluctantly the boy opened his eyes.

'Do thus,' she insisted, somehow managing to make her voice strong and peremptory and slowly he obeyed. 'You are not a coward,' she told him, whispering now, 'you are very brave. And I am not a witch, Malanga. I am not a witch.'

He could not stop shivering and he would not speak.

'We are safe now. The people have gone. They believe we are in the river.' But that was the wrong thing to say because he was afraid of the river and truly believed it was peopled by long-haired half-human entities. 'Come,' she soothed, 'already I feel stronger. We are going to the river to drink water. There I will prove to you that I am mightier than any who may dwell in it. I will prove to you that you have no need to fear.'

Without objection, completely subdued, he followed her: the point of the assegai was no longer required to bend him to her will. Where the long grass ended she peered out cautiously: the kraal was a confusion of milling forms but she had been right, no one had had the courage to remain near the water. She slipped forward, right to the glittering coldness of the river, and scooped water and drank, and scooped water again and held her hands for Malanga to drink, which he did, making sucking noises; and then she held up her arms to the river, and her left shoulder throbbed, and in her right hand she waved the spear, but prudently in case it could be seen from the kraal. Perhaps, she thought, I am descended from a line of great black chiefs, and then she called, 'Come and harm me if you can! I am not afraid of what dwells in the water. If you are strong, show Malanga. Show Malanga that you can do me harm. Accept my challenge and kill me *now*,' and while she waited in the silence, despite herself, a trickle of fear brought a tremor to her limbs, and the boy moaned.

'Harm me. Kill me!' she flung at the river.

The wind ruffled the reeds and the sun, stronger now and warmer, glinted on the bright water, and the tall grass whispered a gentle susurrus; a benediction of peace fell upon her and she laughed.

'You see, Malanga? You see?'

For the first time he spoke. 'InKosazana!' and again, even more humbly, 'InKosazana! Daughter of the

Chief!'

'Let us now go down to the sea for the sea is related to the river and will be even kinder to us. You know the way. The easiest way. I will follow you, Malanga. I depend upon you. Here, take the assegai. UMalanga unomkhonto. Malanga has the spear. You are the man and must be the defender.'

She held out the assegai and slowly he grasped it and would have stood up.

'Not yet,' she warned, 'we crawl until we are completely out of sight.'

'You are a woman to marvel at,' Malanga told her, and the sun's rays warmed him and his shivering was no longer uncontrollable.

'It is the power of the spirit I told you about,' she replied, and wanted to say that the spirit should be thanked, but knew not of any word in his language which would convey her meaning. 'It is the spirit,' she repeated, and said reverently, 'InKosi! Chief!'

A bright flutter of insects flirted over them and she said gaily, 'Izimvemvane Ziyandiza.'

'Butterflies they fly,' Malanga agreed gravely.

'Izimvemvane ezinhle eziluhlaza,' Thola added.

'Butterflies beautiful green,' Malanga said stolidly.

'You have no eye for beauty,' Thola laughed. The butterflies, undoubtedly, were a good omen. 'Forward, my infant. Let us find the sea.'

3

THEY reached the sea sooner than she had expected but had to return upriver some distance before the water was sweet enough to drink. Malanga now looked to her dumbly, as if she truly were some mighty magician whose art could magically conjure up food and shelter; if only he knew how painful her arm had become and how she longed for him to be strong enough and wise enough for her to depend upon him. Too weary to string together the words of his language and stumblingly explain to him, she began to talk in her own language. She had to marshal her thoughts and, in speaking out aloud, she had the illusion that part of her was wisdom, directing the course of another part which was built to go its instinctive ways but not to reason. Each part, it appeared to her, was utterly dependent on the other: what was not flesh – that part that planned and thought – was powerless without the body to serve it. Dimly she felt that thirst was of the body-self, not the wisdom-self, and pain also, and hunger and weariness. And she sensed that some change was taking place in her: maybe the slave had awakened to freedom: thrust on her own resources she acted instead of waiting to be commanded. Wild animals could kill, so could hunger and thirst and cold but, for the present, there was no one who could say, 'Do this!' and make her obey. She was completely and utterly and joyously her own mistress.

'Malanga,' she cried, laughter making her superb teeth flash against the darkness of her skin, 'Malanga, you are now the one who is commanded. But I will not turn you into a slave. I will consult you and consider you and even follow your advice.'

At the sound of the strange words, spoken in a voice bright with happiness, Malanga sat down as a show of respect: he kept his knees up, his whole stance proclaiming his ability to be instantly on the defence. For the first time Thola touched him; she put out a hand and gave him a friendly, sisterly pat on his shoulder, smiling as she did so, and sat down too.

'My friend,' she said, speaking gently and kindly so that even though he did not understand her he was not alarmed, 'somehow you have to use that assegai and spear a rabbit or some such creature for us. And you will have to show me how to start a fire – unless you have a fire perpetually in your kraal – one that dates back to the beginning of the world – and kept alive since so that the art of making fire is forgotten. But I must not go on and on, thinking and talking nonsense, just because of my relief. I must plan.' Thola grinned at the boy. 'I am almost one of you. See how modestly I am sitting. The kraal women taught me. See how I keep my legs together and rest upon them. A woman, after all, is not expected to be ready to fight in a matter of seconds.'

'InKosazana,' Malanga murmured, hoarse with respect.

'We must have food, my brave little, as you would say in your language. It is much like French there. We must have something in which to carry water in case rivers are far between. It is no use asking you. Let us go down to the sea again and search for mussels.'

Once she saw a fat, sluggish-looking snake evilly regarding her from the river bank but she did not remark on it to Malanga; he, like the rest of his people, was superstitious about snakes and considered that these reptiles were vehicles for the spirits of ancestors. After a

35

Chief died a snake was awaited and at the appearance of one some ceremony was performed. She had heard the women in the kraal speak of this.

The wreck of the slaver was visible; had she been able to swim she could have ventured out and perhaps retrieved articles which would be of great use; but she could not swim and she had heard tales of great fish with vicious teeth who fed upon those who stupidly risked their lives in the salt water. There was also the possibility that others from the slaver had been washed ashore and she did not want to linger too long in the vicinity of the wreck. The area around the mouth of the river seemed desolate of human life but she was aware of an urgent desire to get away towards the east.

They found mussels in the rocks and ate, without enjoyment; and then, Malanga in her wake, she wandered farther down the shore, poking amongst the rocks which formed a bank for some distance, and found a piece of wreckage half buried in the sand. Several stout nails were embedded in it, their tapering ends protruding dangerously; at least she had secured an extra weapon. And then, to her infinite delight, she discovered a small wine cask, still securely sealed, the wood blackened by the salt sea-water. Here, indeed, was a receptacle for water.

'I have found medicine from the house that floated on the water,' she told Malanga, 'very strong medicine. I do not think sea-water has got in; if it has not we can drink this medicine instead of water, but we must be careful to drink only a little.'

Malanga looked quickly away from the cask.

'Do you know how to make a fire?' Thola asked hopefully, and the boy explained that two sticks were required; the smaller stick was inserted into a depression made in the bigger one and rotated very rapidly. This was done upon a layer of dried grass. Scrapings from the sticks fell upon the grass and sometimes the scrapings had the power to bring a red glow to the grass; a gentle fanning would cause the glow to burst into a flame.

Thola listened in silence and then groaned; better, for the moment, not to think of the darkness of night. The flow of the sea was ebbing and now she could discern larger portions of the slaver rising above the retreating water; almost it looked as if she could walk across to the wreck, but she did not over-estimate her powers. At the river mouth the water seemed shallower too and she went to the edge of the bank and peered anxiously down, but the muddiness obscured vision.

It is the year 1824, Thola told herself. I am about twenty-five years old, and lost on the southern shores of Africa.

'Give me your assegai,' she commanded and poked it down into the opaque river and estimated that the water would come to their waists – at that point anyway. If only she could balance the cask of wine on her head the way the kraal women balanced water pots.

She decided to watch the line made by the water on the shore and attempt to ford the river when the sea was at its lowest ebb; fortunately it seemed as if silt had formed a sand bank at the river mouth.

The great shadow of Tshaka seemed to loom over her and a quiver of excitement shook her.

When she judged that the moment had arrived she beckoned to Malanga. 'We will now cross the river,' she said; at his start of fear she gripped his arm and pulled him forward impatiently. By now he was so convinced of her magical powers and so in fear of them that he offered no resistance. Steadily she pressed forward; the water swirled around her waist and she summoned all her strength and held the cask of wine above her head; the pain in her shoulder came in waves and her heart

37

laboured. The slimy feel of mud sucked at her feet and once she nearly lost her balance; then the water line fell sharply. As if in a somnambulistic trance Malanga, breathing hoarsely, staggered at her side.

They rested on the opposite bank and to Malanga it was a saying of farewell to the country he had known most of his life. Thola wondered if he thought in sadness of his mother and father and Hlalisa but did not ask. The pain in her shoulder was almost unbearable but the wound, fortunately, did not bleed overmuch.

'Thus we will cross all rivers,' she told Malanga when she decided that he had had sufficient time to come to terms with sorrow and resign himself to separation from the familiar. 'When we see people we will try and avoid them but, if we cannot, we will say that Tshaka waits for us. We will use his name, I think, for our safety, for if it is true that he is so much feared none will have the courage to harm us. When we reach him you will say you have run away to join his regiments and that I am one of your tribe who also wished to be taken into his people. You will never say that I came from the sea or that I speak in a strange tongue.'

The boy, hardly hearing her, sat on his haunches and panted.

'While we follow the sea we can always find mussels. We have the strong medicine in the cask to allay our thirst between rivers, and as we walk we will look for sticks to make fire. Tonight we will sleep in a tree with a fire near. Are there fierce animals that climb trees?'

Malanga described a spotted, cat-like creature to her but she remained undisturbed. Her destiny somehow held more for her than the swift stroke of claws and sharp teeth.

She could not say what distance they had travelled but in the late afternoon she judged it expedient to find a strong tree and set about the business of making a fire.

Danger seemed remote: while they had walked along the golden shore they had not seen any wild animals nor had they heard strange sounds except for the calling of birds. Even now as they moved inland and searched for and found a huge, flat-topped tree and wandered around collecting wood nothing came to disturb them.

Soon enough it was obvious that the wood was too soft to provide enough resistance to spark a fire; in any case the grass was green and succulent. Malanga found a bush and muttered that its fruit could be eaten and together they plucked the red berries, laying them in a heap beneath the tree. They made poor eating but, short of rummaging for more mussels, there was no hope of other food. Thola used a nail from the piece of wreckage to open the wine cask and then tilted the cask and let a little wine run into her mouth and the wine was sweet and heady and warmed her immediately.

'Cup your hands and catch the medicine and drink,' she commanded Malanga and he obeyed.

'Hau!' he exclaimed a little later, his black eyes very bright.

'Now tilt the cask for me,' she commanded. Afterwards she sealed the opening with a wad of grass and welcomed the languor stealing along her limbs. Then she ordered the boy to climb up the tree and settle himself and rest; perhaps it was advisable that one should sleep while the other kept watch. He worked himself into a comfortable position in a fork of the tree, giggled, began drowsily to sing a repetitive refrain and presently fell laxly against the tree-trunk and started snoring softly.

Thola took his assegai and practised throwing it and never once did it land where she wished it to; her shoulder throbbed and the African sun began to lose itself behind the hills. The greyness of evening came and gently shrouded bush and tree and hill; and mists arose, weaving along the ground in ghostly tendrils. Thola pushed the assegai up into the tree and climbed up after it and winced in pain; she wedged herself in beside Malanga and the blackness of night descended and obscured all that lay beneath and around her. Malanga continued snoring and she assured herself of his safety and prayed that he would not move around too much and fall out of the tree. Stars sparked into life and presently the moon, as red as a flame, rose above the sea and gradually became a huge golden globe and then silver, and smaller in size; it laid a spell of white moonlight upon the countryside.

After all, she did not wake Malanga for his watch; she sensed that he would be too stricken by the unearthly quality of the moon upon the unfamiliar terrain and become again a child numbed with fear. Not that she was fearless herself; when stealthy movements disturbed the long grass and ominous sounds whispered towards her her body responded with animal tautness and her skin prickled and crawled; and at a sudden snarling cry she almost sobbed. But at last weariness displaced terror and she dozed, woke up again, and fell dreamlessly asleep.

The temperature dropped but the night was still warm; dew came silently until every blade of grass caught fire from the moon; everywhere sighs and rustles hinted at hidden movement and black shadows coalesced into loping black shapes and in the distance hyenas laughed obscenely.

There was no quietness in Africa: could one have gathered up all the muted whisperings, the sudden snarls, the litany as grass bent beneath changing winds, the creak of swaying branches in trees, the delicate chatter of water rippling over river-stones, the sound of skilful animal attack and desperate retreat, the accumulated blast of noise would have shattered eardrums and toppled stone buildings.

When the sun rose magically out of the sea, sweeping the greenness with warmth, many of the sounds ceased as the night creatures sought sleep; Thola, responding to the golden brightness on her face, opened her eyes and instinctively remained as motionless as a figure carved from stone. In her dreams she had been far from Africa and her mind flinched from the process of orienting itself again to her nakedness and the loneliness around her. Her fingers which, a moment ago, had been touching wine-coloured velvet, fell away from the smoothness of her arm where the skin was puffy because of her wound; and awareness driving away the last, lingering fragment of her dream, she looked for Malanga. His mouth hung open and there was a pinched blueness about his nostrils and his position seemed dangerously precarious. Carefully Thola wedged herself closer and tighter against the tree and with utmost gentleness encircled his body and murmured his name; very quietly in case he awoke with a start that sent him spinning to the ground below. He moaned and whimpered and then peered at her, his face contracting with a child's anxious grimace.

Perhaps the sun's rays evoked the sudden exhilaration in her.

'Malanga,' she laughed, 'Uyasibisa!'

'Who calls us?' Malanga asked, bewildered.

'Tshaka,' Thola said. 'Tshaka!'

4

On the fourth day the wine was finished and Thola filled the little cask with water from the river they had just forded. Surprisingly the wound in her shoulder had healed to a great extent, leaving her arm a little stiff; but, at least, movement no longer subjected her to pain.

Malanga was, if anything, wearier than she. Thola reflected sombrely that she should have chosen a man to accompany her to Tshaka, not a boy; or if a boy, then not a misfit like Malanga, who had a sensitivity quite out of keeping with what one expected in a savage. He lived, it seemed, in a state of constant terror, not only of the dangers around him but of her as well. His servility robbed him not only of initiative but of endurance too. She thought, in exasperation, that very little more was needed and he would simply die of fright.

Yet, despite her exhaustion, an exultation, perhaps a madness, filled her. She had not the smallest doubt that she would somehow pierce the wilderness and beat a path to where Tshaka cast his shadow upon his country; beyond that her mind refused to venture; for the present it was enough to have that achievement occupy her life's horizon.

Her former life was daily becoming more obscured in the mists of forgetfulness and she startled Malanga into terrified rigidity by suddenly breaking into joyous laughter.

'What,' she said to Malanga, 'you are even afraid of laughter? I am gay because I am free. Really free.'

A bull elephant, darkly huge, shouldered his way

massively through the trees; behind him lumbered several other males. Malanga, when he could speak, told her that had the direction of the wind been reversed the elephants would have thundered down upon them and destroyed them. Thola learned that the female elephants, once new life came to their wombs, departed from the males and foraged in a separate troop. Their long period of gestation surprised her.

Imitating Malanga's habitual expression she gasped, 'Hau! I am glad I am not a mother elephant,' and a reluctant grin flickered across the boy's face.

'We had better get on,' she said and did not have to simulate courage. 'Surely we are not so far away from Tshaka's country any more?'

Malanga did not know and shivered at the sound of the king's name.

'Oh, but you are a fool!' Thola cried impatiently. 'Already you fear what has not even happened yet. I do not have to throw bones like that old woman who wanted me for her daughter. I know you will become one of Tshaka's greatest warriors. And I – Malanga, I have thought very carefully what you must say to Tshaka about me. You will say I am a very wise woman. You will tell how I lived in the hills and spoke with spirits when I was still a child. I spoke so much to them that I became halt in the ordinary language of man. You will say the spirits commanded me to go to Tshaka who is the greatest king in the world. Perhaps he is not without vanity.'

The boy's eyes evaded her glance and he swallowed loudly.

In the next river they came upon a great hippopotamus wallowing in the mud, his enormous, distended nostrils giving the impression that his huge head was deformed. Here indeed was a true representative of the river-people, Thola thought glumly. Malanga said the hippopotamus could submerge for lengthy periods and not drown and Thola became helpless with laughter. She could picture the bulky creature, long hair floating from its ugly scalp, singing romantically to itself as it trudged about beneath the surface of the water. The beast looked harmless but Malanga cautioned her, and then licked his lips hungrily.

'It is no use,' Thola said, her dark eyes glinting, 'even I could not kill that monstrosity. Besides, we have no fire. Either we are not skilful enough or the wood is too soft. Anyway, we cannot cross here. We will have to walk up the river and find a shallow ford.'

Malanga was not eager to leave the shore but she prodded him playfully in his back and he stumbled forward.

Higher up Malanga, amazingly, came to life and speared a rabbit.

'You are boy clever very,' she teased him; he would have torn the little animal to pieces and gobbled it down at a sitting, but she would not let him. 'Go slowly,' she warned, 'or your stomach will rebel and you will lose all you have eaten.'

Even in his desperate hunger he was obedient.

'More and more,' she said, speaking to herself, 'I am convinced that I have descended from a line of mighty black kings,' and she bit into redness and rawness and knew no revulsion.

They forded the river with difficulty and had she the gift she would have sung a paean to her God, for it was narrow at the place of crossing and dotted with huge boulders; when monstrous reptiles slithered off the banks she did not pause to satisfy her curiosity but ran with Malanga and, in fact, outstripped him. Once again on the shore of the sea she tossed danger away.

'Oh, stop shivering,' she spat at the boy. 'Do you think to find crocodiles here?'

44

He was prepared to believe that they could fly and when vultures wheeled overhead he was convinced that death was waiting for them; and when a bird screeched over them he read dreadful omens into the occurrence and seemed ready to lie down and surrender. Thola wished she still had wine to instil false courage into him.

'You would not like it if you were bewitched,' she said to him, 'so that you must live near that river for-ever. And all through your endless life a crocodile eats you. Well then, walk!' But when the sun began its downward journey she relented and explained that it was impossible to cast such a spell; in any case, Malanga looked close to losing what little he had left of his control.

Again they slept in a tree and the crimson sky of sun-set was made even more awesome by a roar, fortunately in the distance, which proclaimed the presence of lion; they heard the echoing cough of a leopard and the hyenas kept up their crazy mirth: mad things, they seemed, slobbering and laughing at the edge of an open grave. She wondered if these were different hyenas or whether she and Malanga were being followed with stealthy patience.

For the past two days the vegetation had undergone a subtle change; a sharper greenness coloured what was now dense undergrowth, and even the trees had a different shape and many had fruit, like wild figs, which could be eaten, although she was afflicted at first by severe, shooting pains in her stomach. Surely here, if leaves were bruised, sap would run like blood, and the grasses and plants seemed turgid and swollen; the air was warm and laden with moisture and perspiration glissaded down her body all the time; suddenly she was aware of a new alertness in her and watched where she placed her feet, anticipating often the repulsive feel of

45

slithering coils against her skin. Exhaustion had now perhaps plucked all reserves of strength and progress could only be made by crawling on hands and feet; and she saw that there was a greyness on Malanga's black skin, as if he had been smeared with rice-powder. This was something she had seen amongst slaves and it betokened starvation and killing weariness.

No longer had she the strength to speak encouragingly to Malanga; then, suddenly, she saw the smoke spiralling up into the aching brightness of the sky; inland, but not many miles away. Malanga knelt, transfixed.

'Can this be Tshaka's kraal?' she whispered. As usual Malanga did not know.

'Come,' Thola ordered and reluctantly Malanga followed her, fear roughening his already hoarse breathing. They crept along and eventually the bitter smell of burning wood was in their nostrils and then, unbearably, the odour of roasting meat. Malanga opened his mouth and Thola clapped her hand over his slavering lips and motioned for him to be silent. She abandoned the wine cask but pressed the assegai hard into Malanga's palm and on her belly slithered forward, heedless now of snakes or other dangers. She was on higher ground and could look down: below her were semi-naked men and women, not too many, not what one would expect of Tshaka's might. No cattle were about and no domesticated animals, and few children; the huts were poorly and raggedly made. A great sound of moaning was lifted by the wind and flung towards her; she peered down anxiously in the direction of that hollow complaining. Two men and a woman lay helplessly on the ground near the largest hut and there was something about their pain-racked movements that reminded her of the bull which had been sacrificed in the kraal of Malanga's people. She did not have to be close enough to discern the sweat of fear to know that if ever terror and agony had claimed victims, these three were such victims. The woman began to scream piercingly and a man emerged out of one of the huts and kicked her in her mouth; that Thola had seen happen before in civilised lands and she was not over-dismayed.

'Why do you not stand upon your legs and run away?' the newcomer taunted, his speech so similar to that of Malanga's people that it was easily understood. 'There is no one here to restrict you. For a day and a night you have lain here, dragging yourselves from one spot to the other.' He kicked again and laughed.

In civilisation the feet that kicked were booted; this man's feet were bare.

The woman moaned and the sound seemed to echo back from tree and bush; and her voice was the voice of all who are helpless against the fury of pain. Roughly the man pulled the woman to her feet, but there was no strength in her; her legs were broken and could not support her or . . .

'Oh, my God!' Thola cried; the woman was hamstrung, the tendons at her ankles completely severed.

'Run, maiden,' the man commanded, 'run, for we are hungry.'

Malanga started convulsively and burrowed his face in the tangled grass.

Try as she might Thola could not look away. The man dragged the woman towards a hut and others gathered around him; a heavy club swung through the air with a malignant hissing swish and the woman died.

Most hideously of all, when the odour of cooking meat again drifted up hunger cramped her stomach and even in her nausea she shared Malanga's rampant craving for food. She forced the thought away and concentrated fiercely on her plight. How could she and Malanga escape the cannibals? Were they living in a temporary

47

kraal or were they established? Perhaps they operated from this spot and sent out scouts and hunters for human food.

'Are they Tshaka's people?' she whispered to Malanga. 'Answer me!' When he did not reply she dug her fingers into his shoulder and threatened to pinch him, which she warned would make him cry out and then all would be lost.

'I have heard that many have become eaters of human flesh,' he said at last, his voice catching in his throat. 'Tshaka took their cattle and destroyed their crops and killed their young men – or took them into his regiments. Those who escaped his warriors fled from his might and—' He sighed and quivered.

'Well, be sure then we are still far from Tshaka. Who would dare live like this near him? Unless he too is a cannibal. Does he eat human flesh?'

'For medicine,' Malanga faltered, 'for medicine perhaps.'

'We will have to crawl backwards,' Thola ordered, coming to a decision, 'and try to get away from here as quickly as possible. Keep your eyes open all the time. Whatever you do, keep silent. If you see a snake just let it bite you. God's teeth, Malanga . . .' and she sought for words and finished the sentence in her own language, 'you take everything so literally.'

The next moment there was a slight tremble in the ground beneath them and on the crest of the hill a nebulous cloud of dust rose into the air; from out the dust charged several large buck; the animals, apparently terror-stricken, raced forward, deviated and crashed into dense undergrowth. Then tall feathers appeared, nodding and swaying, and black shoulders and huge shields; within seconds a contingent of warriors loped down upon the cannibals. Over this valley in Africa rang a war-cry, thrice repeated; the mighty reverberations gathered echoes from the surrounding hills and thundered up to meet the drifting clouds dreaming lazily in the glazed blueness of the sky.

Thola was hardly aware of Malanga sobbing at her side.

Very swiftly the cannibals died, men and women; the children's brains spattered the ground. The captives, alone, welcomed death.

But for one man, he who was the leader of the cannibals, death was long in coming: the stick used for stirring the cooking-pot was thrust up him until it penetrated his bowels. He was then left for a while and his howling and screaming were a distortion of sound that bore no resemblance to anything human. Presently a grass mat was carried out of one of the huts and tied around him, and the mat was set alight and he was thrown into his hut and the entrance barricaded.

Thola, confusedly suffering for one who had caused suffering to others, wept with relief when his shrieking stopped: the fierce agony of flames licking the body to a quick death was better than prolonged torture.

Soon enough only burnt-out huts and broken utensils remained of the cannibal kraal; there was a sickness in Thola's stomach and each breath of smoke-laden air increased her nausea. Malanga lay as if dead; indeed she would have taken him for dead had he not shuddered convulsively again and again.

She stared down at Tshaka's magnificent warriors; their black bodies gleamed against the dark green foliage and the sunlight was molten upon their oiled skins and capriciously gay on assegai blades, so that streaks of light sped from spear to spear; their plumed head-dresses danced with every movement in a gentle hilarity quite out of keeping with their ferocious aspect; and their great white shields, marked with almost identical patches of black, threw ominous shadows upon the smoking desolation behind them. Their strong, male voices thundered out the tongue of the AmaZulu; sometimes the words were expelled so explosively that she could not catch their meaning, but here and there a phrase reached her and she was much comforted at expressions of horror against the cannibals.

She underwent a great struggle with herself: here was a way of getting to Tshaka in safety, with food in her belly and Malanga's, and a regiment of spears as protection; on the other hand, the warriors might decide that she and Malanga were members of the cannibal band. Had Malanga been a grown man the situation would have been different, but to jeopardise his life wantonly went against her. Certainly she had led him towards death in that wild flight from his people, but then she had had little choice: he might have been tortured and killed in a hideous way. She had the right to risk her own life, but not his.

The matter was taken out of her hands.

Without warning a party of warriors advanced towards the spot where she and Malanga lay hidden in the tangled undergrowth: not by intent, that was obvious. Apparently a decision had been reached to search the surrounding bush in case members of the cannibal band lingered in the area. For Thola and Malanga there was neither escape nor retreat: in their exhaustion they had no hope of outrunning the warriors. An assegai or one of the short, deadly, stabbing spears would certainly find them.

Thola sobbed once, dryly, in her throat: after the blood-letting she had just witnessed she could command little confidence that the warriors would listen; and in this moment of fear no plan came to spur her onto any effort to discourage the imminence of death. She called Malanga's name faintly and wished he were just a little boy so that she could take him in her arms and comfort him. He raised his head and looked straight at the men agilely leaping up the incline, and jumped to his feet, and Thola, despairingly, pulled herself to her feet and stood close to him and again resisted the impulse to gather him in her arms. He was ashen and his boy's hands trembled; Thola wanted to call out Tshaka's name, as she had planned, but her throat closed up and there was no hope of life left in her. Malanga raised his assegai and she watched, her brain dulled, how it quivered because Malanga's trembling body could not steady itself; and then the boy took a step forward and *threatened the might of Tshaka's seasoned warriors.*

'Come nearer,' he called out, in a high cracked voice, 'and I will kill you!'

The warriors had paused at the sight of the two wavering at the top of the slope and now amusement leapt into their black eyes.

'Oh, Malanga!' Thola wept, suddenly so fiercely proud of him, and somehow it seemed he was her own flesh and blood. Now that she was inescapably in the presence of death panic was overcome and she felt her heart exult because of the boy and his impossible courage. 'You are a man,' she shouted, 'more than any before you.' Her voice gathered strength and unconsciously she followed a pattern as ancient in its tradition as Africa itself. 'You are a defender who is braver than the mightiest.' She wanted to sing the words; she wanted to scatter echoes from where the sea began to where it ended; her pride was so great that she felt as powerful as Tshaka; as if she could destroy the flower of his army with her bare hands. 'This is a wonder that a child has the courage of a man. Look at him, Tshaka's warriors: look at my defender. I would rather die with Malanga as my defender than live with you as my protectors. Oh, Malanga, Malanga, Malanga!' and her voice made his name reverberate, and she startled the birds in the

51

trees. 'My brother. Malanga,' she continued and began to laugh with sheer, proud joy, 'you are all courage. You are my brother and I love you,' and, suddenly, forgotten words returned to her and in her own language she said, 'Yea, though I walk through the valley of the shadow of death, I will fear no evil' and the words had true meaning for her, and she believed them, and they were like a song of high courage. Death had not yet come; the men with their black skins and plumed head-dresses and mighty shields were staring up at her and Malanga in wonderment. Inspiration came and she said to them, 'We are not cannibals. We have journeyed far to reach Tshaka.'

At the sound of that name a murmur broke the warriors' stillness.

'He' – she touched Malanga's shoulder gently and he flinched but his assegai remained pointed at the men – 'he longed to join one of Tshaka's regiments – and I – I am a wise woman and saw great things about Tshaka and wished to tell him that all the land belongs to him; every mountain and hill and valley and plain; every river and...'

The warriors rushed forward and Malanga, in his moment of intrepid bravery, did not wait for them but leapt forward and threw his assegai. When a man seized him he struggled with all his strength, his teeth exposed, his thick lips drawn back, but he was a baby struggling against a giant; and Thola, who had not been pinioned, closed her eyes and bent her head and waited.

'Ehe!' a rough male voice said, 'it has the heart of a little lion. Wait! So it wishes to join forces with the mighty elephant. It is not an eater of human flesh the woman says. It has not the look of an eater of human flesh. It is very thin and a bad colour from hunger and its body is much scratched as if it has indeed journeyed far. It is too brave to die!'

'It does not give up, the little man,' said the warrior who had seized Malanga. 'I let my grip go for an instant and it tries again to overthrow me.'

The one who had first spoken suddenly thrust back his head, plumes waving, and burst into laughter; not shrill mirth: a deep, rumbling bass.

'Let him live,' he ordered. 'The Mighty One shall decide his fate.'

The words penetrated Malanga's despair and he raised his hanging head; a smile began to lift his lips. Any minute, Thola thought, he will start boasting and singing his own praises. Her tears had dried and she longed to thank Malanga's saviour but so far, although covert glances had been sent in her direction, no one had commented on her presence; and, now that danger had retreated, she had no excuse to behave improperly by addressing Tshaka's warriors; forwardness on her part would not be fitting. None of the warriors was over-tall; but all of them were lithe and shining with health. Malanga's saviour had a gold – or was it brass? – ring around one arm and looked to be the leader; but he, like the others, was nearly naked.

'Rape?' she wondered, keeping her eyes lowered, and was conscious of her own lack of covering. But she was not a child and had undergone too many hardships to shudder much at the thought of being assaulted; what would rape matter as long as she survived such an onslaught? Peril lay in the fact that Malanga, in his new-found valour, might destroy his chance of life by attempting to defend her again.

'The woman wishes to tell the Great Elephant that this land is his,' the warrior with the brass ring said, and smiled so that the swift flash of white teeth lightened his countenance out of its naturally stern repose; a sternness that certainly belied his propensity towards ready mirth. 'So be it. Come, little one, you have need of food and so has the woman. We return to our military base near the hill that sticks out into the great water. The bulky thing. Do you know it?'

Malanga respectfully shook his head; he seemed to behave with perfect propriety, but then custom had been strictly adhered to in his kraal. 'No, my father,' he murmured.

In truth the earth trembled beneath the stamping feet of Tshaka's warriors, and the dust rose and obscured the sun, and the wild things fled before them. Thola and Malanga staggered in the train, choking in the dust, half dead in their fatigue. But they had not been shackled and no one bothered to ensure that they did not escape. It was a wonderful thing that Malanga's statement had been accepted and no doubts were held that his intentions were good and that his heart lay with Tshaka.

They came to Khangela at nightfall; fires flickered in the dusk and the rounded, crouching shapes of huts enclosed within a palisade could be faintly discerned.

Here Thola found herself in the company of over-hospitable women; she was given a hut and the luxury of a sleeping mat. Her ravenous hunger surrendered to drowsy satiation; fires lightened the darkness with their red glows and increased her sense of well-being and added to her awareness of security and safety. The stars came out and shone upon a superb bay and a high stretch of land that formed a bulwark against the sea.

She was in Tshaka's country.

Tshaka ka Senzangakhona, Tshaka son of Senzangakhona, who was the son of Jama, who was the son of Ndaba, who was the son of Mageba, who was the son of Phunga, who was the son of Zulu.

The name Zulu signified Heaven and from Chief

Zulu a nation derived a right to be called the People of Heaven.

Thus the warriors chanted outside the huts, their voices lifted in izibongo: Izibongo ZenKosi UtShaka Zulu: Songs of Praises to the King, Tshaka Zulu.

A woman called Nandi, which means sweetness, became not the first wife, not the second wife, but the third wife of the Chief of the AmaZulu: Senzangakhona; and Senzangakhona was vassal to the mighty king of the great Mtwetwa tribe, the Old Lion, King Dingiswayo.

Grievous was Nandi's unhappiness at Senzangakhona's Esi-Klebeni kraal; therefore she went from him and took with her their son, Tshaka, and she returned to the home of her father who was of the Langeni tribe; she married a man of the people and by him she had another son: Ngwadi.

Where dwelt content? Even in the Langeni tribe Tshaka, the Small Lion, suffered cruelty; yet his character was so strong and his nature so determined that neither pain nor ridicule succeeded in daunting him; his 'shadow', his personality, was so unusual that others ever surrendered to him.

The Old Lion, Dingiswayo, heard of Tshaka and sent for him, and gave him into the protection of Ngomane, who was the head of Dingiswayo's impis. Tshaka became a great warrior; when he called men to meet the menacing shadow of death in battle he had to turn his head and thunder his voice across his shoulder, for he was always first to approach the enemy. He knew not fear. He earned the Praise Name 'Sigidi', One Who Is the Equal of a Thousand Men, and 'Sidlodlo Sekhandha', the Pride and Honour of the Army.

He was a mighty hunter and with his bare hands he killed a lion; he killed a crocodile; he pitted his strength against the most dangerous of all, iNdlovu, the elephant.

The people murmured their awe; the warriors worshipped him, and the maidens spent long hours dreaming of him; not only was he the bravest of the brave but he was also of a great height and exceedingly good to look upon.

When the father of Tshaka died, one of Tshaka's half-brothers became Chief of the AmaZulu, not Dingane, not Mhlangana, not Umpande, but Sigujana, the son of Bibi, yet Dingiswayo had indicated that he wished Tshaka to rule. Tshaka therefore sent Ngwadi, the son of Nandi, to the AmaZulu and Ngwadi killed the usurper, Chief Sigujana, and Dingiswayo lent Tshaka might and Tshaka claimed the AmaZulu for his own and became Chieftain.

Now Dingiswayo went to war and was treacherously killed, and Tshaka took over the Mtwetwa whom Dingiswayo had ruled, and the Mtwetwa became people of the AmaZulu.

Tshaka dispensed with the old spears and introduced a new weapon, a short stabbing spear, which was never thrown and lost but wielded at close quarters; more than ever a battle became a scene of extensive slaughter.

The king, at the head of his army, conquered tribe after tribe. 'Ngadla,' the warriors cried, as their spears tasted blood, 'I have eaten!'; men, women and children died in their thousands; those whom Tshaka permitted to survive were the ones useful to him, and they became absorbed into the AmaZulu; any element that might at a future date oppose him again he did not spare. When he entered the land of a hostile people even the earth was defeated, for he destroyed all crops, and fired the grass and captured the cattle. Inyakato, Iningizimu, Impumalanga, Intshonalanga, North, South, East, West, he triumphed.

Within the boundaries of the Zulu kingdom prosperity smiled on all; without foreign tribes destroyed and pillaged and brought death and famine upon themselves.

Ah, Tshaka, King of the AmaZulu, unparalleled in valour, famous maker of songs, lithe dancer, powerful hunter, hero of his people, ruler of the world!

Thola listened wonderingly, not always understanding the more obscure phrases; and she realised that she would never fully understand the Zulus, and doubted if she would master their language completely. Not that it was unduly complex. The Zulu tongue was down to earth, much as the old languages must have been before civilisations sprang up: languages that had to do with work, sickness, the essence of existence, life and death. In ancient days when life consisted of killing to eat, killing or being killed, perhaps people did not sit down to admire the landscape; they did not pause breathless over the beauty of a flower; and certainly they did not weep over the death agony of an animal when they had more often to contend with the death agony of a child. In the beginning man lived without artificiality, as did these people. When lightning struck man did not understand and worshipped the phenomenon; when a man fell ill maleficent powers were blamed.

Perhaps her own grandparents had roamed half-naked in steaming jungles and thought of the moon as a platter in the sky and believed that it was cyclically eaten up and regurgitated again.

But the Zulu savages had succoured her and had been touched by Malanga's childish valour, and had not harmed her in any way; in civilised hands she might not have escaped unscathed. Of course, they had not pampered her; she had not been carried nor had anyone treated her with the respect usually accorded to women (at least those who were not slaves) in the country where she had run at her mistress's bidding. But that was of little importance. Here, in this unknown part of Africa, she felt as if she lived close to elemental things; here nature was evident and the breath of nature could be heard in the sighing of the wind.

She would not think too much of Tshaka. He was too near at hand; and a tightness in her throat constrained her breathing when her disobedient mind darted into mazeways of speculation about him.

She slept for a night and a day and another night; then, in the morning, she ate and walked down to the stream and washed, choosing a tree-shaded place below the spot where the men performed their ablutions, for she knew that a man may not bathe in water tainted by a woman's uncleanness. The water in the little river was clear and sweet and brought her skin tingling to life and instilled strength in tired muscles. She crooned as she washed, unafraid now of reptiles: there were none to be seen and the men would have warned her had there been danger. She scooped the crystal water into her hands and drank deeply.

Other women came down to bathe and they were beautiful, and maintained a strict reserve; she was not to discover until she had left the kraal and was on her way to Tshaka that those dwelling in the huts opposite the entrance to the kraal were the pretty ones of Tshaka's isigodlo – a word which she interpreted as seraglio. Whether they were genuinely women for Tshaka's pleasure there was no knowing: she was never to become entirely clear on this point, for these women generally comprised a female regiment and were sometimes given in marriage, Tshaka collecting the lobola cattle. Some of them might have been mere workers, for many went out to hoe and work on the tilled patches of land; they also cooked the meat, beasts chosen from the huge cattle kraal, prepared the amasi or sour milk, which the warriors were not permitted to drink, and brewed the beer, which she soon discovered was an infallible remedy for debilitation: her starved limbs began filling out and the lustre returned to her skin.

Malanga she hardly saw until the day came when she was summarily told by the Chief of the kraal, a woman and a relative of Tshaka's, though in what degree Thola did not know, that scouts were returning to the Great One's kraal.

'You and the boy will go with them,' the woman said authoritatively, and gave Thola cooked meat, a large portion of the rib-cut of an ox, and a woven-grass pot containing a stiff porridge made from crushed maize.

Thola bent her head gratefully, receiving the gifts in her outspread hands and murmured, 'InKosikazi! Wife of the Chief!'

She wanted to enquire about Malanga but the woman walked away haughtily and it was with delight that Thola, a little later, saw Malanga approaching. There was a gloss on his black skin and he walked with a most definite swagger. Thola had to restrain herself otherwise she would have embraced him and kissed him and undoubtedly scandalised the entire kraal with her brazen behaviour; Malanga returned her smile and she saw that his assegai had been returned to him and that he handled it with possessive pride and a new assurance.

A dozen or so magnificent warriors formed into line and then proceeded into the bush, their loping stride agile and graceful; and she and Malanga hurried after them and it was pleasant to be in the train of seasoned men who would probably not even fear an attacking lion. The men continued along some sort of trail which Malanga explained – a trifle breathlessly because of the swift pace – had been made by elephants. Animals always found the best and swiftest routes and such tracks were utilised by the people.

'You are fat,' Thola told him, 'and look well. Tshaka's people treated you as you deserve. Tell me what you talked about.'

'I am not in their age-group,' Malanga whispered back. 'They are grown men and did not have much to do with me but I am praised for my courage. I did great things. I showed no fear,' and his eyes glittered in happy recollection and his stride became even more jaunty; and again Thola longed to kiss him: this boy, now transformed from a stranger who had never been much more than a necessary nuisance into a brother, much loved.

'I shall never forget your courage,' Thola assured him. 'You will become Tshaka's greatest warrior. You have true courage, my friend. Malanga, I love you dearly.'

His swagger increased, to his undoing, and he tripped over tangled vegetation and nearly fell and she was hard put to restrain her laughter.

'Have we far to go, Malanga?' she ventured, when mirth no longer threatened her gravity.

'We shall sleep again and again on the way,' Malanga replied, 'but not always beneath the sky; sometimes we shall be guests in a kraal and receive food. Food is very plentiful; these people do not know what it is to feel hunger. I have told how you cast spells and many have great respect for you. A man does not fear what he can see but he fears all that strikes secretly. To whose spirits do you speak, Thola?'

'I speak to one spirit, Malanga. I do not speak to the spirits of my ancestors, for this spirit is over them.' She knew that Malanga believed that a great spirit broke away from a bed of reeds and from him descended the people. But the Ancient One, Unkulunkulu, was not really worshipped as God; for that he was too distant, perhaps too impersonal: the power, the force behind

60

life and all manifestations of life. The prayers and petitions of the AmaZulu were directed to ancestors who lived in a shadow-world similar to the world they had inhabited before death. Ancestors were entities intimately connected with the living and understanding the problems of the living. There appeared to be no conception of God and Devil: all was God. To him were ascribed no notions of good and evil; evil existed only in whatever caused harm to the community; that which was out of place and upset tradition. Certain things could be done and others could not be done. No ideas were entertained of hell-fires or torture for sins committed; but a vague concept existed that the personality, the shadow-form of the living was immortal; and this shadow-form retained the characteristics which coloured it during life: kindness remained if the person had been so disposed, and brutality remained, or otherwise; power and importance in the land beyond death depended on the power and importance the individual possessed while on earth. Certainly there was no thought that the physical body could be resurrected and again imprison the shadow-form or soul. Thola was suddenly happy to think that in this land, despite its savagery and brutality, no man, woman or child had ever met death with the fear that hell-fire awaited.

She and Malanga jogged along in silence; the men ahead appeared to be tireless and she was reminded of the sweep and movement of magnificent animals in whom strength was so conserved and every action so effortlessly controlled that force was not unnecessarily released or wasted. And even when she was weary and footsore, with her lungs protesting achingly, and the surrounding countryside beginning to swirl and dissolve in the mists of tiredness, she did not complain.

Oh, but it was joy to be alive; to know that all about you were vast spaces where no man had ever set the soles of his feet; to walk as a free woman, owned by no living being, and feel your body hungrily absorb the hot rays of the African sun; to hear the strange call of unknown birds and see their brilliant plumage; to tread upon sweet grass and drink from clear streams; to start at the rustle of animals, just beyond your sight, and know fear, not of the whip, but of nature's unspoilt life; to live where men still lived as they did in the first ages, unfettered by clothes and unconstrained by the perplexing concerns of civilised life; to lie down and rest, the earth itself your bed, so close to the quintessence of existence that the voice of creation spoke: not a deceiving voice, not sophisticated, not hypocritical, a voice that said, 'I give you what I give all. Kill to eat. Be killed to provide sustenance. I erect no screen of false security. I say you live and sleep in danger, but all share this with you. I am life: live. I am death: die.'

And to know that at the end of the journey stood Tshaka: a most magnificent product of nature, a ruler by virtue of innate power, a living proof that he who is closest to nature in that innate power is the survivor. She felt that Tshaka's justice would be nature's justice: he who is not strong, let him die. He who conquers by virtue of strength discovers his own mercy and makes his own rules.

If Tshaka ordered her death and Malanga's, that would be a reasonable gesture: it would follow nature's pattern of logic. A small animal, if it does not develop fleetness, cunning and adequate protective colouring, will not long survive. Brute power develops in what is weak latent protective abilities. In a country where nature ruled what was uselessly weak had to be exterminated. The body, that material envelope which sheathed the soul, could not compete with the sources of power in the material aspect of the world; so fragile a thing it was, surviving only through the ingenuity of a clear intellect.

Yet when nature kills she does so only to give new life: the soul lives on.

'I have strange thoughts,' she told Malanga and he smiled uneasily.

In the red glow of sunset she lay down to sleep and tossed all through the dark hours of rest beneath the stars; from then on the journey became an age of torture. Whether she slept in a kraal, warm in a hut, or in the open with the mad laughter of hyenas on the hillsides, her waking hours were spent in a trance, a semi-conscious state wherein she ate without tasting, hardly spoke to Malanga and could not say how he was bearing up. Her every sense was concentrated on the need to survive, to follow, to endure the strain imposed upon her.

When, at last, she arrived at Tshaka's royal kraal, Bulawayo, she was so drugged by fatigue that she could hardly see; she crawled into a hut and fell asleep in a triumph of delight.

No one disturbed her peace and she slept for a long time and awoke to a world of blazing sunlight, azure skies and somnolent heat.

Malanga, she thought, was probably quartered with the boys of his age-group. The royal kraal was so vast that she would not have found him even if courage had grown sufficiently to permit her to make a search. As it was she remained submissively in her hut, receiving with gratitude the food she was offered. Discretion, she felt, was for the moment her strongest armour.

She was now at the very place from where Tshaka's power cast a shadow as far east as Delagoa Bay. It darkened the waters of the sea washing against those shores named by Da Gama and obscured the sun inland towards the mysterious north; and his shadow sent banners of darkness towards the west where the white man ruled.

On the fourth day after her arrival at Bulawayo the people gathered in a concourse and regiments of warriors milled around and fell into place before the many huts at the far end of the kraal, opposite the entrance.

Cautiously Thola edged out of her hut.

5

TSHAKA stood before his subjects and his servitors brought him fresh raw beef which had been pounded into a salve and he rubbed the red mass over his tremendous limbs; globules of blood, so much more viscous than water, ran down over his great chest; and in the steaming heat of the mid summer morning the blood clotted along his thighs. He was lighter in complexion than many of his people, nevertheless the scarlet blood gleamed richly against the deep, dark brown of his skin, and the sun shimmered hotly upon the smooth hairlessness of his body. Several inches over six feet in height he was, and he cast a long shadow upon the ground.

The people stared in awe at his huge nudity. To his left was an elderly man who had the merest suspicion of a sneer upon his negroid features; perhaps not a sneer, perhaps just the quirk of involuntary fear, but Tshaka Zulu found him repulsive. With his little finger the mighty elephant of the Zulus pointed in the direction of the man and instantly men leapt at him and twisted his neck and he died.

The silence, the intensity of stillness, became achingly oppressive. Water was brought forward, humbly, and Tshaka shook the glittering wetness over himself; and then a herb, which if rubbed, produced foam. The white foam and the coruscating drops of water mingled with the red blood. Lithely and swiftly Tshaka passed his hands over his body and he was awful in the sight of the gathering: a magnificent ruler, a personification of the darkness of earth, of the imperturbability of air in which silver lightning sets the sky ablaze, of the revivifying, malleable, fertile-making power of water, and the triumphant, unsubduable, all-changing potency of fire.

Calabashes of clear water were poured over him and he was approached with a paste made of fat and red ochre, and this he smeared into himself with strong sweeping movements; his skin absorbed the fat, more and more of it, until the eye-searing light seemed to reach him as if focused upon him; a black, velvet-like lambency emanated from convulsing muscles in the lustrous column of his neck and a luminous patina lay upon the breadth of his shoulders.

The sunlight fell upon his head and gleamed around arrogant eyes which had a slight look of the oriental about them, and spilled onto his cheekbones, such harsh planes of strength, and upon his thick, curving nose. He raised his face and his firm lips revealed their autocratic lines; and then the light discovered the determination of his granite chin, and bathed him in golden effulgence; and nowhere, in physical form or features, exposed the slightest weakness.

The man who administered to him during those moments when even a king had to be about his natural body functions stepped back; one who provided Tshaka with emetics submissively handed the king a calabash and Tshaka drank deeply; he received a feather with which he tickled his throat. Soon afterwards the king vomited copiously and violently.

'Bayete! InKosi!' the people shouted. 'Hail, O Chief!'

Dismayed, Thola crept back into her hut. What had she expected? A mere man? An effeminate who overcame nausea in genteel privacy? She had seen someone that was almost a phenomenon of nature: a perfect

66

physical form which emanated a personal magnetism and an aura of indestructible strength; physical beauty made radiant by a boundless inner intelligence. Here was a savage, she told herself, and shivered, who could conquer the continent of Africa; here was a man who, had he been born into the white world beyond the sea, could have accomplished what Napoleon had failed to achieve. She had not even been close to Tshaka, had not heard the words he had spoken, yet that magical vitality in him had already mastered her. He inspired fear and automatic obedience; almost she believed in devil gods incarnate. And yet he did not diffuse evil: he was the centre point, somehow, of an unknown force ...

Malanga and Thola were summoned into Tshaka's presence in the early evening. Fires were glowing redly and the dogs growled around and licked out cooking-pots. Singing and movement came from the faint darkness and watchmen stood stolidly on guard at the entrance to the royal quarters. Even at this hour, so close to sleep, the atmosphere was not relaxed: close proximity to Tshaka strung nerves to breaking point, and subdued laughter did not hide the tension in every heart, yet that tension was full of pride and adoration for the black king.

Tshaka was stretched out in a great hut on skin rugs. Flaming rushes provided a smoky light. Women were present and several men and at Tshaka's feet lay a man who, Thola subsequently discovered, was Tshaka's human footstool and spittoon.

Malanga at her side, Thola crawled into the king's presence; the floor of the hut was like glass and shone but, God knows, it had been formed of cow manure beaten and polished into the hardness of stone; the air was foul and acrid with smoke. Her eyes watered and a tickling arose in her throat and, despite her efforts to stop herself, she sneezed.

67

Instantly absolute silence came; every person in the hut was frozen into immobility, breathing temporarily suspended.

Fear, Thola thought, has an odour, and so has death: the sweet sickliness of decomposition perhaps. And the smell of fear was in her nostrils; also the smell of death.

Malanga gave a faint, a very faint moan, and Thola looked up. Tshaka had raised himself into a sitting position, and she met his eyes, black slits completely expressionless, the oriental slant to the eyelids much intensified. The king's lips were slightly apart, not laxly, but sufficiently open to show the barest glimmer of square, white teeth. The flickering light played on the muscles of his neck and shoulders, and caught the wooden discs in the lobes of his ears; and his massive chest rose and fell, rose and fell, with his unhurried breathing; his hands, long and surprisingly slender, the fingers strangely sensitive, lay relaxed, pink palms upward. Not anywhere upon him was there a cushion of fat; and for all his great size he seemed vital and slim and agile.

The expressionless eyes held her own under mesmeric spell and all the world dissolved into nothingness; and then Tshaka spoke, his thick lips curling away from white, immensely strong teeth; his voice was low enough to remind her of an animal's snarl; not the little animals, the big massive ones, yellow beasts with black manes. The deep voice said abruptly, 'Many have died for less.'

And again she was subjected to the deepest, most minute scrutiny, the oriental eyes flicking over her face and resting on the rigidity of her neck where the muscles were locked, as if in a spasm, from the effort of keeping her head lifted while lying flat before the king.

'Many have died when I was not ready for laughter and something about their features amused me.' He was not trying to frighten her; he was not boasting: flatly he was stating a fact.

'Lord,' Thola whispered, 'I have so often been intimate with death that I no longer fear.'

'Those who do not fear death,' Tshaka replied, watching her narrowly, 'yet fear the manner in which death claims them.'

'That is so,' she agreed. 'But even to pain there is an end and death will at last stop a screaming voice.'

'Only women scream,' Tshaka said sombrely. 'My warriors die praising me.' His inscrutable gaze fastened on the quivering Malanga. 'Perhaps this child who was so brave against my warriors would keep silent.'

'Lord,' Thola said quickly, frantic with sudden terror for Malanga's sake, 'undoubtedly you would never make the slightest sound.' She was horrified at the cutting edge to her voice and Tshaka bent his look upon her again and smiled very slightly. With absolute finality she knew that no torture devised by man or devil would ever succeed in twisting the faintest moan from him.

'The child has a voice, I suppose. Would you scream, dog?'

Malanga muttered into the floor and it was obvious that his terror was so intense that he was already close to screaming.

'He does not fear death,' Thola forced out through numb lips, 'nor does he fear pain. It is you, Lord, who strike terror; your presence strikes terror greater than that inspired by fear of death or fear of pain. There is a power about you, Lord, that is too great for lesser beings. Men, I think, have died just from being near you.'

His laughter was deep and uncompromisingly male.

'One died, indeed, from fright – when I pursued his army in war.'

'Lord, this lad has braved extraordinary dangers out

of devotion evoked by your name. He could face danger but, as you see, you he cannot face.'

A small frown grooved the wide smoothness between the curved black brows. 'Now that he has seen me,' Tshaka said gently, 'undoubtedly his devotion has increased a thousandfold. It must anger him to realise that you talk too much and annoy me. For my sake he should kill you.'

She did not so much see as feel the men in the shadows arch forward in readiness to obey the king's commands.

'It is a hard thing to kill a defenceless woman – and not an honourable deed.' Her throat threatened to lock on her, but she swallowed convulsively and made yet more desperate efforts, and gambled high. 'Should I bring such a thing to one who stood against your soldiers in an effort to save me? Besides, do not deny me the happiness of effecting the removal of what causes you irritation. Permit me to kill myself.'

His eyes caught her again and she did not try to look away. And suddenly a sturdy pride warmed her body and she thought, 'It is true. Death must come at the end. There must be an end to screaming and to pain. And there is more to me than quivering flesh. Life now, after all, is not the greatest prize. Life continues onwards, forever and ever. Shall I cringe before a savage and turn myself into a fear-crazed animal and bring to the dust the glory that enables me to think and move; that causes *these* thoughts to arise? He is a king with complete power in his hands and I was a slave only a little while ago, but I am as much a part of life as he is, and life is a proud thing, and the immortal essence in me is full of pride too and unafraid.' She crawled forward, closer to the king, and whispered so that he alone heard, 'I am not afraid of you. My body you can tear to ribbons and my bones you can crush to fine powder, but my spirit you cannot kill. I believe my spirit will live for always and it is not such a great thing to die, after all. If you make my body cringe, know it is the weakness of the flesh when I plead for mercy. My spirit will be defying you no matter what my tongue may shout.'

'Believe me,' the king said sombrely, 'you will not even be able to whisper.'

Thola stared at the king, and it was madness, but the magic his name had roused became a greater magic now and flooded her with warmth and tenderness. She resisted the impulse to put out a hand and touch him; and the madness grew and intensified so that, with death already cold upon her, gaiety yet lifted her heart, and she found herself smiling, and tears came to her eyes, and she said softly, 'Lord, indeed you are a man. Do with me as you will for I love you greatly.'

In the huge hut there was no sound save rustling murmurs from the burning reeds. Tshaka's heavy lips folded together and the frown deepened; he took a pinch of snuff, but his gaze never wavered.

'Bring nearer the puppy who admires me so extravagantly,' he ordered. 'Tell me of your travels, boy,' and a sigh floated around the hut, and taut muscles relaxed and the flames from the burning rushes shot higher.

Now Thola left Malanga to speak; he kept his eyes lowered and his mouth trembled; then, gradually, a little confidence returned to him, and he began to glow with enthusiasm as he described their adventures; when his story reached the point of their meeting with Tshaka's regiment he faltered and fell silent.

'So you defied my dogs,' Tshaka observed gently.

'Lord of Blackness,' Malanga stammered, 'I was a fool.'

'A fool indeed,' Tshaka said; he looked down at the boy and suddenly he smiled and a brightness came, as if the dark heavens had been conquered by the golden light of the sun, 'but a brave fool. Yet I do not believe

that admiration for me spurred you on to leave your
people. You have told discreet lies – but let that rest.
Those who have high courage should, whenever possible, die in battle; courage earns that reward. Puppies
sometimes have very sharp teeth. You shall bite for me,
small dog. You shall become a child of Heaven.'

Now Malanga's delight was so excessive that it was
laughter-provoking. He could not speak and in his
happiness he wept with joy.

'Ah,' said Tshaka, 'you did not weep at the thought
of death. But you quivered as rapidly as the shake of
birds' wings in flight.' Harshly he called a name and a
man leapt forward and knelt. 'See that this boy is
trained. He may be taken into the boys' regiment.
From time to time' – and the smile lightened his face
again – 'remind me of his existence. Go!'

His eyes flicked around the hut. 'All of you,' he
said, 'go!'

This command, Thola soon realised, did not cover
his human footstool nor the servant who kept the fire.

'Bring light here,' Tshaka added, and the man crept
forward and Tshaka bent and lifted Thola's face so that
the red radiance from the flames spilled over her forehead and cheeks; then the king sat back and motioned
for her to rise and she did so. Suddenly he reached forward and touched her. In the presence of witnesses she
was embarrassed and moved back, startled.

'And you love a lad,' Tshaka said.

'Malanga is a brother to me,' she whispered, half
fainting.

'Come here,' the deep, bass voice ordered. Her limbs
suddenly so heavy that they were a burden, she dragged
herself to him and fell on her knees and again the king's
hand took her chin and lifted her head. The fingers were
warm and gentle and the thought came to her that he
could have been as mighty a power for good as he was

for evil. 'Are you truly evil? Are you as cruel as men say?' she wanted to ask, and knew immediately that he was neither good nor evil; more, he was a personification of that affliction which life produces now and again, an impersonal product of nature which, by its mode of life, brings out greatness in those who suffer under such a scourge.

'You are a forward woman,' Tshaka told her, and she thought that the teasing rumble in the deepness of his voice was the fruit of her imagination, 'and you have a sharp tongue and an agile mind. I am of the opinion that you have more courage than that puppy whom you love so much that you would rather kill yourself than have him kill you.'

'It is not that I love him so much, Lord, although I have a deep affection for him. But he did a wonderful thing for me. I do not wish any man to have to redden his hands with my blood.'

'He would not have to redden his hands. He could take your neck – like – this,' and the long fingers fastened around her throat in a vice-like grip and she knew that hardly any exertion would be required to choke the life out of her body, 'and twist.' But instead of fear peace came to her, and a feeling of security: with this man she was safe against all danger. She let her cheek fall against his hand. 'Give the word and it shall be done,' he said, and his shadow loomed over her and her cheek pulsed against his arm.

'I am truly not afraid to die,' she murmured, unconsciously rubbing that pulsing cheek against his hand. 'The first time I heard your name I was bewitched. It is a strange thing that your name is nothing without you – an ordinary word – which you have turned into a thing of might. As long as the black men of Africa live that ordinary word will have enchantment – always it will mean supreme authority. It is strange, is it not, Lord?'

'Do not love this Malanga too much,' the deep voice said above her head, 'for I have in mind to make you one of my sisters,' and the grip relaxed on her throat and the long, sensitive fingers wandered over her cheeks and touched her lips caressingly. Abruptly he released her. 'Remove that matted hair. You have offered no information and I will not ask questions. Take my sister to her new home,' he ordered, and his footstool darted out and within seconds a servant entered. 'My sister is weary and seeks her sleeping-mat,' the king continued. 'Escort her to her hut and return with others to comfort me.' He paused, and the smile returned, and he named several women, and the servant grovelled.

Thola went with a furious heart. She was not tired and the king knew this. But for Tshaka women were not matters of great importance: he had his appetites under iron control. Food and drink were necessary but not ends in themselves; women were a source of pleasure but existence was not arid without them: even his desire for blood was the result of the vision he held of an unconquerable Zulu nation. She entered the isigodlo, perversely angry despite the fact that her life no longer hung in balance. Then the thought came that had he been indifferent he would have kept her with him and used her – casually. Could it be possible that she had impressed him so much that he now sought to impress her? No, that was moon-madness. Tshaka would not stoop; it would not even occur to him to seek to impress.

The guards around the isigodlo were an ugly, scowling lot: ill-looking, all of them, to the point of deformity, yet not deformed but so wrought that the lines of their bodies departed greatly from what was beautiful. Tshaka, then, did not feel that his women would remain faithful just for the love of him. Did his women truly love him?

The hut she entered was, by ordinary standards

74

and particularly by the standards of Malanga's people, the last word in luxury: large, no airier than that of the poorest dog of Tshaka, but stoutly fashioned, with great sleeping-mats and thick animal skins, silky smooth; and around this particular hut were grouped other huts, the quarters of Tshaka's sisters, over five hundred of them in this one kraal; all of them beautiful and fresh and probably largely virginal. If she expected jealous glances, these she did not receive; curiosity indeed impelled the women's eyes towards her, but not jealousy. Excitedly some of the women went off to Tshaka's hut; six at a time, Thola thought dryly. Perhaps the king did not regard them as human and therefore was unconcerned that they would witness his every action. The idea disturbed her: she remembered tales of slaves whose mistresses walked naked before them as if they were pet animals.

What criterion of beauty ruled amongst the Ama-Zulu, she wondered. She was so slender in comparison to the other women. They seemed to go in at the back, in their waists, and their stomachs protruded so that they had the slant of women far advanced in pregnancy; yet their tubby, shining limbs, the grace of their movements, their proud carriage and their beautiful breasts – not large, but smooth and rounded with youth – gave them a delightful loveliness. Apart from little bead aprons, bead decorations, brass rings and small feathers in their crinkly hair, they were in a state of shining nakedness. Their bodies were glossy and satiny and utterly hairless and their bright black eyes were quick to gather laughter-glints, and she never saw one with malformed or decayed teeth.

Uncertain among them, no word as yet addressed to her, she looked down at herself: her legs were long and slim, whereas they, although tall some of them, seemed to have rather short legs and long trunks; her arms, though not thin, were not plump and her stomach was flat, her back straight, and her waist very small. Servitude with white people had somehow bred out black African characteristics; perhaps an Arab strain had given her a straight nose and thin, supple lips.

Then Thola saw a woman who was certainly her senior, regal as a queen, and with compassionate eyes and gentle features. Around her neck were brass rings, so tight against her skin that she could not turn her head; she was lavishly decorated with beads, and more rings gleamed against the blackness of her arms. Subsequently Thola discovered that the brass rings were marks of special favour.

'Come,' the woman said to Thola, 'my sister.'

6

THOLA was in the anomalous position of being
Tshaka's concubine – as were the other women – and
yet he could accept the bride-price from one of his
subjects for her and marry her off if he wished; she was
in his isigodlo for his pleasure – and yet she was in a
female regiment attached to the kraal, as were other
regiments attached to every one of his kraals; she was
an unmarried woman but she could be treated as a wife
and deflowered, when, in all the kingdom, no man might
deflower a woman without marriage, and adultery was
punished by death. Of course, according to Tshaka, she
and the others were his 'sisters'. Some of those with her
prepared his food; others did a certain amount of work
in the fields, and all of them delighted the king with
their singing and dancing.

'The Black One might give permission to one of his
regiments to marry,' her gentle friend told her, 'and
direct them to choose their wives from one or another of
the female regiments.'

'And if they want to marry men in other regiments?'
Thola asked.

'We are happy to do the Black One's bidding,' the
woman replied evasively and lowered her eyes. She
turned and winced, and Thola saw the raw redness at
the side of her neck; the sore seemed to run in under the
brass rings which circled her throat.

'That must be painful,' Thola said, wincing in sympathy, 'you will have to take the rings off and let the
sore heal. How did you hurt yourself like that?'

'The rings often cause this soreness. It will go away again,' and the woman dismissed such trifling pain. 'It is now time for you to go and draw water with the others. I will show you.'

'And you? Are you going to draw water too?'

'I do not have to work. There are some of us on whom the king smiles. Perhaps you will join us too. Of course the royal ones do no work. They have their maids of honour. You are very beautiful.'

'I will never be as beautiful as you. I have not your gentleness. How shall I manage with the water? I cannot balance a pot on my head.'

This occasioned some surprise and several girls stared curiously; one, a little spiteful thing, muttered that idleness had no reward. Women welcomed additions, not only in the isigodlo, but in the homes of ordinary people as well; extra hands meant less work and most women worked hard.

'Carry your pot on your head and help it to balance with your hands,' UmuSa, Thola's friend, whispered. 'Do not fill it and then you will be able to hold it easily. This is a strange thing that you cannot balance a pot.'

'My mother was a wise woman and lived mostly in the hills gathering herbs for medicine,' Thola said. 'I did not live with the people very much. Sometimes we slept for long periods in a cave and lived on berries and food that grew beneath the ground. I am very stupid in the ways of the kraal.'

'You will learn, my sister.'

Thola, last in the line, walked with the girls, and watched their swaying hips and the proud way they had of carrying their heads high, and reflected that she, with just a few beads covering her thighs, was a pauper among them, for they were all plentifully decorated with beads, some having what looked like bibs of beads depending from their necks. They sang as they walked

78

and there were giggles and even a few malicious remarks addressed for her ears; but on the whole they seemed happy enough and kind enough.

When they returned to the kraal there was much bustle and activity; presently Tshaka emerged from his great hut and seated himself before the isigodlo and his barber shaved him. He had several counsellors with him and he talked and turned his head, the barber hovering agitatedly over him. In the morning light Tshaka seemed even more exceptional: too masculine, steel-strong. Once or twice he yawned prodigiously and noisily, those around him murmuring inaudibly as he did so. When he moved his head the muscles rippled in his neck and danced in his shoulder-blades; and again it seemed as if the rays from the sun were caught in a focal point upon him.

A crowd had gathered and now and again his eyes flicked over the assembled people, flicked like the sting of a lash; and clouds moved over the sun and the wind blew cold. He jerked his head to make some remark to a counsellor on his left and a little blood, a small spot, appeared at the side of his forehead; the barber gasped and froze and a great sigh swept over the concourse.

What followed was Thola's introduction into the nightmare of Tshaka's world: the king touched the bleeding spot and looked at the blood on his fingers and a moody blackness fell on his face and his flickering eyes grew still and expressionless; then his tigerish lips curled away from white teeth and he growled out a short, staccato order. Men leapt forward and within seconds the barber was dead, his neck broken. And suddenly, without apparent reason, the long, sensitive fingers pointed here and there, again and again, and men died with little grunts, so quickly that they scarcely had time for surprise.

A stillness descended upon the women, a rigidity that

only relaxed when minutes passed without further death. A servant took the shavings of the king's hair and went into the isigodlo and burnt the shavings; and, as if he were handing over a burnt offering, gave the container with its powdery contents to another who departed immediately and carefully threw every atom into the river.

The women of his harem had the king's food prepared and UmuSa whispered to Thola, 'The Great Black One desires you to be present when he eats.' A look of compassion was on her face, as if she anticipated some catastrophe for Thola and Thola became aware of a feeling of nausea. 'We have made the porridge as he wished; the Great One's cook has prepared the other food.'

Thola crawled into Tshaka's hut; he sat aloofly on his skin rugs and did not glance her way; his cook, a fat man with a ring on his head, a black, waxed affair which she later discovered betokened the married man, arrived at the head of other carriers and reverently placed before the king a dish of broiled meat and a calabash of amasi, sour milk. At the entrance to the hut a pair of crossed hoes indicated that the king was at his meal, and silence lay heavily on the kraal.

Thola had no idea how to serve and she waited dumbly; the king stared down sombrely and gave no indication of his desires; the inceku retreated respectfully, perhaps for other dishes, and Thola gave a very slight cough to attract the king's attention and Tshaka's head jerked up.

'You surely wish to die,' he said, his voice very benign.

She stared at him blankly, whispered, 'I am a stranger to the ways of your people. What have I done?'

'I will forgive you for coughing in my presence,' Tshaka said. 'Another would have died. But I will forgive no more. Be silent in all things.'

She retreated from the vindictiveness in his eyes and the inceku returned and Tshaka ate; and he was an animal, tearing at the meat so that the red juices ran down his chin; and his fingers became greasy, and he stuffed in more than his mouth could hold, and his teeth ground noisily; and when he motioned towards a pot and she, understanding him, held the beer for him to drink, he spluttered and slurped, and the nausea in her stomach twisted into great knots. Yet, for a man of his size, he ate sparingly. And in comparison to what she had seen of Malanga's people and Tshaka's own people, he ate daintily.

'Are you hungry?' he asked her, his tones peremptory.

'No, Lord,' she stammered, and swallowed.

'Nevertheless, you shall eat.' He plucked at a piece of meat and she caught an agitated murmur from the inceku, a whisper advising her to lie down. On her belly, her neck straining up, she had to force herself to swallow the meat which the inceku had taken from Tshaka. The inceku offered her great gobs and she summoned every vestige of will-power and managed not to choke; despite the stress imposed by her position she ate delicately, keeping her mouth closed while she chewed.

'Do not be an ill omen to my kraal,' Tshaka said and touched the little spot where the barber had cut into his skin. 'Have you had enough?'

'My Lord's bounty has over-filled me,' she answered, and tried not to gag.

'Leave me now,' Tshaka ordered, 'but come to me tonight.'

The air outside steadied her and she drew its sweetness into her lungs and wiped at her mouth with her hands. UmuSa came to her and told her that she had been singularly honoured.

Now Tshaka performed his ablutions in the sight of his people and they were suitably awed by his physical beauty; and then he walked, with stately tread, to a huge chair carved out of wood. A man stood behind him and held a tremendous shield over him to protect him from the burning rays of the sun which was already gathering fierceness on its path across the blue glitter of the heavens. Other men grouped around him and a servant knelt nearby with a container of snuff and Tshaka gave instructions and listened to reports.

Afterwards the king danced with his warriors and the dust rose and thickened the sky and drifted in the wind. It was a dancing like nothing known: a stamping of feet and twisting of body, and movements executed as if in battle fray; and hundreds of male voices chanted and the king, apparently no mean poet and singer, sang in his deep bass rumble; and the red feather on his head dipped and swayed, as if immersing itself in the blood with which he had stained his land.

Next a great parade of cattle took place. Vast numbers of beasts, divided into various colours: white herds first, then brown, red, dappled and black herds. The king looked on his wealth; the people chanted and saluted him; and the hoofs struck up more clouds of dust; and the chanting, the lowing, the stamping, the activity, the frenetic excitement, all gathered and created an intangible atmosphere of stress and tension as if hidden forces played in great, black rain clouds and would soon unleash tremendous shafts of lightning and blister what was below in a death of fire.

Again, for no apparent reason, the king pointed a finger and one, two, three men died; they died uncomplainingly, those with a few minutes' grace praising the king.

Thola, stunned by the noise and the hideousness of sudden death, half-heartedly looked around for Malanga, but he was not to be seen; in any case, he could have been anywhere in the excited, swaying masses.

She lived through the day in a somnambulistic trance, scarcely conscious of those around her, and UmuSa whispered, 'You are quiet, my sister.'

'I am dazed by the king's magnificence,' Thola replied and shuddered.

Tshaka sent for her, and several others, early enough: the stars were faint in the evening sky and there was no moon. Silence settled over the great kraal, though here and there singing arose; and in the huts fires glowed. The sentries around the women's huts moved stolidly, and at the entrance to the kraal guards kept their eyes trained on the external world, ready to advance upon any enemy foolhardy enough to threaten Tshaka's peace. Hyenas laughed crazily and that mad sound was characteristic of Africa, far more so than the roar of lion or the trumpeting of elephant. Strange, unfamiliar whispers wafted from the darkened countryside and cattle lowed complainingly; a little child wept and women's voices sang sweet lullabies; and there was an illusion of simplicity and gentleness and quietness upon all.

Tshaka's hut was dim with smoke from the fire and warm; and the smoke made Thola's eyes water and tickled her throat. She crawled in after the other women and emulated their reverent greeting. The king was, as always, attended by men, and at his nod they withdrew. Still not speaking, he motioned to Thola and with another silent gesture indicated to her companions to remain beyond the light of the fire; then he commanded them to sing, which they did, very softly, with a note of longing in their voices which Thola found hard to interpret.

This time the king drew her onto the softness of the skin blankets and the pelts were smooth against her bare skin; and she sat modestly, her legs crooked at the knees and folded back under her; and Tshaka's massive shoulders were only inches away from her; and his black, inscrutable eyes flicked over her with their whiplash intensity.

'You have nothing of your own,' he remarked after a while and touched her little apron of beads, and she drew back, startled. 'You shall have many beads and cattle, my sister, for I look upon you with favour. It is a madness, I think, for you are a very forward woman. Also you are not a young girl but a woman of maturity. Are you a maiden?'

'I am, Lord. And I am bowed down under your generosity.'

'So it seems,' he observed dryly. Abruptly he shouted a name and a girl rushed forward. 'Has this one been deflowered?' he asked, nodding at Thola. 'Let your eyes discover for me.'

Thola's body went rigid with shock, so that she did not even think of protesting; the girl straightened herself, then popped down on her haunches and whispered, 'She is virgin, Black One,' and crawled away as his hand pointed to the shadows beyond the firelight.

'That is well.' Tshaka's hand came up again; fascinated, Thola watched the long sensitive fingers and shivered as they caressed her neck. 'Here you shall have rings,' Tshaka said. 'You journeyed far to come to me and I am pleased that you undertook that journey. For, in truth, you wished to come to me. You shall not leave me again. You have now been here nights and days, my sister . . .' and the fingers explored her shoulders and returned to her throat, and very gently stroked her cheeks and lips and slid over the hollows in her temples and started once more on their downward caress. A heaviness came to her, and suddenly her arms were seized and she was pinioned against him; and even now his breathing was even and she felt the strong beat of

84

his heart in his great chest; and in a swooning dimness she found herself pleading, 'But the others . . .' and he asked, very low, 'What others?'

'The women . . .' she sighed, her eyes closed.

'Dogs,' he said, and the terrible strength of his heartbeat quickened, 'dogs, beauty of maturity,' and his presence shut out the soft singing, the flickering firelight and the entire world, and his gentleness was unbelievable.

She awoke to hushed singing and the same warm firelight and listened to the sound of strong, unhurried breathing; and she stirred and the tremendous weight across her arm stirred too and she looked up into Tshaka's eyes.

'If I have a child . . .' she thought, and found herself drowsily speaking out her thoughts, and Tshaka, as awake as if he had not slept at all, said, 'There will be no child.'

'But,' she protested, 'but there *must* be a child.'

'Shall a maiden have a child?' he asked her, and now his voice and eyes mocked her and a slight smile twisted his lips.

'Maiden?' she repeated, her voice rising. 'That is not possible. I know.'

'You know nothing. Prove for yourself.'

She could only stare at him.

'It is easily proved,' Tshaka told her. 'Come, satisfy yourself.'

'When I am alone,' she said, turning her head towards the darkness where the women crooned, and she felt warm blood rise into her neck and face.

'You are a strange one,' and the fingers caressingly turned her head back. 'Tshaka does not have children, flower of maturity. You shall not be exposed to the stress of pregnancy and the knowledge that the child will die – and you too perhaps.'

'Are they all . . .?' she asked, turning back to the women and his deep laughter mocked her.

'What is a dog's life?' he demanded. 'For my pleasure they lose their children – and sometimes their lives, when they are stubborn. But you, amongst others, shall not.'

'All men desire children,' she insisted. 'Sons.'

'Kings, particularly Tshaka, cannot afford to have children. I am in the process of forming and building a very great nation; the country needs a ruler who is not plagued by jealous sons. When sons are in the kraal they scheme and seek to devise death for their father so that they may rule. I know for I was a son, although I did not remain long in my father's kraal. His people have greatly repented the shortness of my stay with them.'

'But surely you want a son of your blood to rule after you?'

'For the moment Tshaka rules forever,' he replied shortly.

'Then perhaps you will want children from the woman you love.'

'Dadewet-u!' he exclaimed, 'May I sleep with my sister! You are truly a forward woman. I love the woman who bore me, Maturity. I love my country most jealously, and my people. You, I think, I also love. But I will have no children and I will have no gainsaying. I am the law and the law stands first and all other things come afterward. And no man or women is essential to me – not even you – although I would miss your going.'

'You say you love your people,' Thola whispered, steeling herself against the hand that caressed and fondled her so gently, 'yet I saw how you had them killed.'

'Some die so that others may live,' he told her, a slightly impatient note in his deep voice. 'They are expendable and you will do well not to be so concerned over them. My purpose requires instant obedience and absolute fear: cattle understand the voice of authority; dogs do not bark at their master.'

'Perhaps you will also have me killed.'

'That may happen,' and Thola saw, starkly, that if he found it necessary she would indeed die.

His hands released her. 'Sleep there,' he commanded, pointing towards the edge of the rug; suddenly afraid she crawled over. Then he summoned one of the women, a young, plump and pretty girl, and the warmth of the fire-light flickered over Thola and over Tshaka and the girl.

Thola nearly cried out; she did, indeed, cover her face with her trembling hands and moan, abjectly wondering whether she had now become nothing to Tshaka: a dog whose presence as a witness was of little importance, an insentient thing like the pillar in the hut. She rebelled against the outrage he was forcing upon her and the tenderness he had evoked in her was swamped by fierce hatred, which in turn was overwhelmed by a resurgence of love and a possessiveness which shook her in its jealousy. She was infinitely shocked by his iron control; had that control endured with her too, while she, like the foolish girl now in his arms, became lost to reality? Her mouth filled with the unpleasantness of bitter herbs.

His country, his people, his women, and she, oh, most completely, she belonged to him, and he, Tshaka ka Senzangakhona, King of the AmaZulu, the great Bull Elephant, the Mighty Yellow Lion, the Black One Who Endures Forever, he belonged to no one.

He had forgotten her and she was desolate, and in her desolation she wept softly into the skin blanket; then hands gently pulled her forward and warm lips whispered against her wet cheeks, 'You should sleep, little

87

one. Soon the light of morning will appear and each day holds its own sorrows,' and, almost with the soft, comforting touch of a woman's hands, her tears were wiped away.

Oh, I am no longer a woman, a person, a being, she wailed to herself, surrendering to the consolation his action had brought her. I am not Thola; I am now truly a slave, more than I ever was before. I am a thing, a toy for Tshaka. And involuntarily her lips touched his arm and she fell deeply asleep.

The other women Tshaka commanded to return to their quarters, but Thola he left near him, and for a long while he sat beside her, gazing down at her; and his face was expressionless.

The light from the fire gleamed upon the cruel arch of his nose and the red glitter of the flames drew no response from his black eyes, and no man knew what was in his head.

And no man knew what were his thoughts.

Presently he covered the sleeping woman and once, with feather lightness, touched the soft lines of her lips.

Then he lay back, his face towards the fire, and looked into the leaping flames.

The night became very still.

7

THEN the white men came and she cringed back into the shadows of her hut, afraid; but reason eventually convinced her that no one would venture into Africa's wilderness in search of one female slave, or any slave, particularly after a shipwreck. Covertly she watched the white men approach and was much impressed by a tall, chubby-faced, slightly whiskered, young man who apparently was a friend to Tshaka, for the king greeted him with pleasure. Gifts were handed out to the Black One, and Thola was immensely pleased that he, a savage and unused to white products, could so conduct himself that dignity overcame curiosity. Tshaka remained a king throughout.

She did not then appreciate the chubby-faced man's courage, but in after years discovered his true history. His name was Henry Francis Fynn and he was in his early twenties: a trader, much interested in ivory. Previously he and his companions had sailed up the coast and had anchored in Delagoa Bay; that voyage had been made in the hope of bartering with the Portuguese; Fynn was then supercargo of a sailing vessel *Jane*. He spent six months in the area and here it was that he first heard of Tshaka whom the local natives feared exceedingly.

Fynn now returned to Cape Town where he joined forces with a Lieutenant Farewell and a Lieutenant King, who had returned from an unsuccessful voyage down the coast; indeed, not far from Delagoa Bay they had met disaster in a river, three men being drowned;

their interpreter, a black man called Jacob, escaped, made his way to Tshaka and became one of his dogs.

From Cape Town Fynn returned to Tshaka's domains in the sloop *Julia* and landed in what was later to be known as Port Natal. He found starving natives and desolation, but managed to communicate with Tshaka and after an interval was taken to the king who took this courageous white man to his heart, and gave him royal protection. During a subsequent visit an attempt was made to assassinate the king; Tshaka was wounded and Fynn doctored him to the best of his ability, and Tshaka made a grant of land to the traders who owned F. G. Farewell and Company. The tyrant of the Ama-Zulu and the young Englishman had become firm friends.

And now Fynn was back; and Tshaka watched him narrowly; and around him were thousands upon thousands of Tshaka's warriors, vivid in their war regalia; and Tshaka and his warriors danced for Fynn, a most magnificent spectacle; and women regiments danced; and then cattle were driven past, again thousands upon thousands; and the royal women danced; and the sun advanced in the brilliant sky.

And Tshaka dwarfed the assembly.

And it was a day of great slaughter: men died to the left and to the right. One moment they were staring in adoration at their ruler, if not relaxed, at least not anticipating death; and the next moment they were rushed off to be executed: a twist to their necks or the swing of a heavy club. No one resisted; all died praising their king so that even in this last trial, this greatest of all tests, their loyalty was unshakeable. Again and again Tshaka's fingers pointed and each time he spoke the crowd thundered out the royal salute. 'Bayete!' and the vultures wheeled, 'Bayete, InKosi!' and the wild terrain of Africa echoed the tremendous cry. 'Bring your enemies, our Father, and let us eat them for you. Hail, our Chief. Hail, Father!'

Tshaka's oriental eyes flickered from face to face: he was at his most gentle. A slight smile played around his lips and the red bird-feather swayed above his head and fluttered in the feeble wind; and with his smallest movement his muscles rippled and the sheen of his dark skin caught the sun.

Then somewhere in the great concourse of people one of the little boys, the small ones who acted as carriers to the warriors, snickered, perhaps in hysteria, perhaps with the irrepressible irresponsibility of childhood. And several other childish sniggers intermingled with Tshaka's deep tones as he spoke with the white man. The king looked up; his mouth grew taught; and then that gentle smile came widely and a magnanimity settled upon his features.

With joy Thola thought, 'He does not mind. He forgives children.'

But the people, watching Tshaka's alert expression, fell silent; so silent that the whisper of grass could be heard; or perhaps it was the frail whisper of inhibited breathing.

'Who laughs?' Tshaka asked of one of his counsellors, a very tall, swarthy man, much in the king's favour.

The man sank on his haunches before the king. 'It is perhaps the wind,' he ventured, 'perhaps it is the wind that praised the Black One.'

'Ah,' said Tshaka, and the smile broadened, 'if I did not love you so well those ears which heard badly would be removed, and that tongue which spoke lies would be plucked out. Send a dog to see. The laughter came from over there,' and with that long-fingered, sensitive hand he pointed.

A warrior ran to do the king's bidding and the people parted and the breathless hush grew achingly oppressive; and Tshaka continued to smile with great benevolence. The warrior returned and squatted reverently. 'Only children are there, Great Elephant. Only the carriers of the mats – and there is no laughter on their faces.'

'Your eyesight fails me,' Tshaka murmured gently. 'Remove his eyes so that he may learn that Tshaka needs eyes which see with a sharp clarity.'

Men leaped upon the warrior: he did not struggle, nor did he scream.

'Great is my chief!' he called in his strong voice. 'It is good that my chief possesses himself of my eyes,' and, as the blood streamed down his cheeks where pain had grooved furrows, he called again, 'May he live long, my father!'

Fynn and his companions, their pallor extreme, moved restlessly.

'Bid those who have children among the gibers to come forward,' Tshaka commanded.

They came swiftly and there was a trembling in their limbs; and they bent before the king.

'Slay your children,' Tshaka murmured and smiled benignly upon them.

A woman wailed once: such a stark sound, sending such agony to the heavens.

'Bring the children who drown my words with their bird-chatter and insolent laughter,' Tshaka said; and warriors ran to the little boys and shepherded them forward as if they were little calves; and those who had sons amongst the carriers groaned and tears ran down their cheeks and their hands hung slackly and their bodies were without strength.

'Lord,' said one man, older than the rest, 'I love my son dearly but I love my king more. I do your will, Black One,' and he went to kill his child, his head bowed.

And now Thola was half mad: why did the people permit such horror? Tshaka was one man, and thousands of men were grouped around him; they could rend him to pieces. Surely he was only flesh and blood. And then she saw that the king was weeping, and that a look of intense suffering had settled upon him; and suddenly she remembered that whenever he commanded death to come to one of his people that expression of intolerable sorrow had aged his face, and that, at the moment of death, he had always turned his head away.

'Stay!' he called after the man. 'Indeed you love me truly and death is not for those who obey my wishes. To you I say that my most earnest wish is this: the mighty AmaZulu shall rule the earth and all its nations. You shall live and so shall your son that he may become a favoured warrior. This land will have need of him. Take your child and lead him away from the others,' and Tshaka waited until this was done, the old man's praises ringing about him, and then he said, harshly, 'For the rest: let them die!'

A small boy screamed sharply, but for all of them death came with swiftness; and Tshaka turned his attention on the recalcitrant fathers. 'As for these,' he said, 'ensure that they sire no more children.' And he watched the men being hustled away and sat in silence until the footsteps faded. 'Now bring to me the woman who screamed.'

She was not a young woman and she was half-crazed with fear and grovelled in the dust and wailed piteously and pleaded that she had only this one child: this flame of brightness in a dark world, this small boy who was now dead. Fynn, unable to endure the tragedy, whispered to Tshaka and the king looked aloofly at the white man and then smiled that terrible smile. 'Since it is your wish,' he said, 'she shall not have her blood shed. She is a dog who barks against the commands of

93

her master, but she shall not be clubbed, nor shall a knife spill blood, nor an assegai pierce her. For your sake.' And the king issued another command: 'Take her to her hut and secure her there.'

The woman, realising that death had retreated, babbled incoherently in her gratitude and, intermixed with her praises, were her mad lamentations for her son, the flower of her life, the warmth of her hearth.

From then on there was thunderous dancing again and another review of superb cattle; and later eating and drinking; and when the whole kraal sat down to eat the sound grated unpleasantly on fastidious ears.

A blood-red sunset came and then twilight panoplied the early night sky in pastel colours, cool apple-greens and mauve-blues; and suddenly, like the swift pulling of a black, velvet curtain, darkness fell and the stars appeared in bursts of cold, diamond glitter; and a spurious tranquillity absorbed the placid lowing of cattle and the muted resonance of voices; orange and crimson spearheads of flames from a myriad little fires pierced the gloom, and the distressed crying of small children was hushed by the comforting, crooning intonation of lullabies.

Tshaka had the white men brought to his hut and he sent for Thola and others and he lolled on his skin rugs and asked many questions of the white men.

Thola, although the hut was warm, shivered in the shadows and listened to the king's deep bass voice as he explored the white men's minds, and she was astonished at the swiftness of his intelligence; still, he was naïvely intrigued by the white men's King George and demanded to know whether the English king had sons. Fynn, obviously at a loss where the First Gentleman of Europe was concerned, muttered evasively that the Georgian majesty had many brothers and, certainly, children.

'He is a fool then,' Tshaka announced. 'Children cause dissension, particularly sons. They will plot against his life,' and he listened with quiet amusement as Fynn insisted that in King George's country sons did not plan to kill their fathers.

'Yet it is so,' Tshaka observed. 'The desire is black in their hearts. Perhaps they scheme to destroy him in a woman's way. With poison. Their eyes are on him and they covet his power. He would do well to kill his children and preserve his life,' and Fynn's chubby face registered such a degree of horror that Thola, despite the nausea caused by the day's slaughter, nearly laughed. 'There are many in my kingdom who seek to destroy me. Envy is always present. You – with your white skins – covet greatly. You want, I think, my country.'

Fynn hastened to assure the king that all the white men wanted to do was to trade; Tshaka's land was his alone.

'That is so,' Tshaka agreed heavily. 'While I live this land is mine and all in it. And while I live, despite your guns, you who cast envious looks at my possessions will be driven into the sea from whence you came. I do not say that you personally desire my country. I think you are an honourable man, my finch with the black tail. If all white men are of your calibre then I did right in commanding my people ever to treat those with white skins with respect and reverence. Am I right in thinking that all who are unfortunate possessors of white skins are like you, Fynn?'

Fynn dropped his eyes and looked singularly uncomfortable.

'I have in mind that when I am gone and the riches of my country are discovered your people across the sea will stretch out greedy hands and seek to grasp this land and deprive my people of their heritage. For my children are simple; only the king, their father, can keep them secure. There is perhaps a slyness in white minds. Therefore I must live until I have strengthened the dogs of Tshaka so that they can stand invincible against the cunning and the might of the white men.' He stared sombrely into the leaping fire.

Thola thought, 'Ah, Lord, you do not know it, but white men bow down to the money a man has – often – and not to the man himself. They bow down to the past glories implicit in a name that a fool carries. But your people do not bow down because of your wealth of cattle; they do not bow down because of your power; they do not remember an ancestral name; they bow down to you – the man.'

'I see that you still have not brought me the Oil of Life, my finch with the black tail. It may be that you do not wish me to have it, thinking that should I die you will easily help your king to possess himself of my land, my warriors, my cattle and my women.'

'No, indeed,' Fynn said quickly, hiding his little spurt of sophisticated amusement. 'We have sent for the oil and are waiting impatiently for it to be brought to us. We have sent to our country beyond the seas for it.'

'Perhaps your King George wishes to keep it for his sole use. That is understandable.'

'He would be excessively pleased for you to have it,' Fynn put in and again a glint of laughter enlivened his plump features.

'Hlambamanzi who fought an enemy in the spirit world for me,' said Tshaka, irony tinging his voice, 'is not of that opinion.'

An agile man nodded respectfully. He was the man, Thola saw, about whom the women in the isigodlo had told her. He had lived with white men but had not been happy in their company and while acting as their interpreter had escaped during a boating accident and swum to safety. He had fled to Tshaka, and had told Tshaka many devious things about life with the Abelungu, the white people.

'We are greater in all things. Is it so, Swimmer?'

'The Black One has said it,' the man murmured and kept his eyes lowered and Fynn made a little gesture of impatience.

'Tomorrow,' Tshaka announced, suddenly changing the subject, 'we shall hunt.'

When the white men left to go to the huts allocated to them, he kept Thola back; and again he stared sombrely into the fire, oblivious to the smoke which bit into her eyes and made them water.

'This oil,' he muttered, 'it is necessary to procure this oil. But the white men evade me. There is some conspiracy to deprive me of it, but I will have it.'

'What is the oil, Lord?' Thola asked, greatly aware of his nearness yet relieved that he did not touch her: in the firelight there was a look about him as if blood lay upon his skin, and the killing and horror of the day was vivid in her mind.

'Oil of Macassar,' Tshaka replied, his tongue slipping with difficulty around the strange word. 'This oil keeps the white from the hair and thus must be a method of retaining the fires of youth.'

So great a king, Thola thought, and so ruthless, holding the power of life and death in his beautiful hands, and as naïve as a child; or as ignorant as a child. But only because of unfamiliarity. Place him amongst whites, a white man, and he would truly overrun the world. Already, like Alexander, he was complaining he had little left to conquer. Did he realise how far the continent of Africa stretched to the north; did he give thought to other savage peoples; to deserts that would have to be crossed; to the turbulence of great rivers that would have to be forded; to snow-topped heights of mountains that challenged the might of that heaven from which he had his name? Discreetly she said nothing.

'It is not that I fear to die,' he said, and he was speaking to himself; it would not have occurred to Tshaka to justify himself to anyone, least of all a woman. 'But my death will leave this country defenceless. It will be taken, every piece of it. It will groan beneath strange ways, desolate in strange hands. When I have subdued all and have formed one great nation, then may death be my end. Until then Tshaka is needed. Without me there will be squabbling and a breaking up and a fighting of tribe against tribe. My country will break into pieces like the shards of a broken pot, and crumble and blow away as dust in the wind. Therefore there must be no dissension; no one against me, neither counsellor nor warrior, neither women nor children.'

'Yet,' Thola said, suddenly afraid for him, tenderness returning despite the memory of a day of terror, 'there are your brothers. You refuse to have children yet you allow your half-brothers, Dingane and Mhlangana, to live. Is there no danger there?'

The king looked up at her alertly, aware now of her presence, and the slow, lazy smile illumined his face. 'The woman who bore me has warned me of them too,' he said, and then added contemptuously, 'I do not fear women!'

'They are not women but envious men,' Thola dared to say.

'They are the sons of my father. I will not bring competitors into the world but I will not kill the sons of my father.'

'And today so many died,' Thola said, unable to stop herself despite her fear of incurring his displeasure, 'so many.'

'That is good,' he said shortly. 'It is well for the white men to know that Tshaka commands instant obedience and that he shows no mercy. They will think before they attempt to endanger his country.'

'But children,' Thola said and looked straight up at him, meeting his eyes, and he did not flinch.

'Children made a point which adults may not have made. Let the children mock and get away with it and perhaps the grown men will try.'

'I do not think the children mocked. I think they were afraid and ...'

'They died and it is done. You are an extremely forward woman, flower of maturity. When the flower blooms in a covered recess the petals have a long life of loveliness, but if the flower is exposed to strong winds the petals are dispersed and the stem is snapped.'

'It must be wearying to have everyone always agreeing with you, Lord,' she said, uncowed, and suddenly he laughed and pulled her against him and began to caress her with practised skill; and as much as she longed to resist him, her body failed her; and not just her body, but her heart too, for love made an agony within her: a yearning and a tenderness, a compassion, an adoration that was a searing pain.

And she was achingly humiliated when he seemed to tire of her within a few minutes of caressing her cheeks and neck and bade her return to the other women waiting in the shadows at the far end of the kraal. But at least he called no other to his side.

She watched the firelight play on him and once he passed a long, beautiful hand over his face and she saw that his cheeks were wet with tears and that there were more tears in his eyes.

'He remembers the children,' she thought brokenly and wept; not now for those who had died, but because of Tshaka's lonely desolation.

The hunt next day was all excitement and Tshaka went off with his warriors and the white men. He was resplendent in his bead decorations and his kilt of monkey tails and the skins of genets; the monkey tails were not truly tails from the animals but skins twisted in a clever way to simulate the effect. Around his arms were semi-gauntlets of ox-tail, and further ox-tail bunches ornamented his legs; and from his neck hung a monkey and genet-skin garland. The red feathers on his head swayed and dipped with each stride he took and the white men seemed pallid and insignificant beneath their burden of clothes.

At evenfall the party returned laden with carcasses of animals; the women of the kraal set about their business of cooking, and general merry-making followed. The warriors chanted and above their song rose the deep bass of Tshaka's magnificent voice.

Later, at ease on his skin rugs, Tshaka spoke again with the white men.

'You killed many animals today with your spitters-of-death,' he said gently. 'To whom do they belong?'

Fynn's hand went up to his mouth to hide a smile. 'To you, of course,' he said. 'We are your guests.'

'No; they are yours,' the king said and laughed. 'You are a man after my own heart, Fynn.'

But on Fynn's next visit tragedy came for Tshaka. His grandmother had arrived from her kraal to visit him and Thola had been amazed at his deep love for the old woman. He had taken her trembling, wrinkled hands and with great patience and care cut the nails for her; and with utmost gentleness he had cleaned her ears and her eyes; and she had sat with him for meals; often, tenderly, he had put choice morsels in her mouth and sighed at her toothlessness and palsied weakness.

'Ah, my oldest love,' Thola had heard him murmur, 'strength must return to these limbs. I cannot bear to see you so,' and his deep voice had had the softness of a woman's tones when she comforts a small child.

Then she fell ill and Tshaka asked Fynn to see to her; by this time she was already mumblingly raving in a delirium of fever and the tall white man reluctantly told the king that death was upon the old woman.

Late at night while Tshaka was conversing with Fynn in the royal hut a servant crawled in and announced that the Old One had gone home; the king stared before him, his features set; the minutes passed and the whole kraal was caught up in an intensity of silence. Then the king put his hands over his face and wept; and his people wept with him and cried aloud their sorrow; and his people sang and throughout the night all lamented and throughout the following day and sadness enveloped the land of the AmaZulu.

The white men returned to their settlement at the bay where the long ridge of land jutted out into the water; and behind this crouching bulwark the waters of the bay lapped serenely.

8

AND at the royal kraal one of the huts gave off a fearful stench, and when it was opened the woman for whom Fynn had pleaded was found, or what remained of her was found; and she had been scraping at the cow-dung floor for food, but had starved and thirsted to death.

'Ah, God,' Thola whispered to herself, sickened; and she looked blindly at UmuSa. 'She was forgotten!'

'That is the way of death for those who do not have their blood shed,' UmuSa said. 'She was not forgotten.'

'But the white man . . .'

'The promise made to the white man was kept,' and UmuSa's tone of voice plainly indicated that she did not wish to pursue the subject. Unthinkingly she tried to turn her head and her enflamed neck caused her great pain.

'I wish you would remove those rings,' Thola pleaded. 'That festering sore is increasing in size.'

'The Black One honoured me with the rings,' UmuSa said. 'I must wear them.'

'But if you explained to him . . .'

'Do not let us talk of the king,' UmuSa put in quickly.

'No one can hear us.' Thola saw that the gentle swelling of early pregnancy was visible in UmuSa, and would soon be obvious to all.

'The walls of the hut have ears and the grass sighs with many tongues.' UmuSa dropped her eyes and stood in silence for a moment and then whispered, 'Did you know that the Black One will soon go forth to eat up his enemies?'

'Is there anyone left to stand against him?' Thola asked bitterly.

'The brother of the son of Zwide is here. It was the tribe of the Ndwandwe who killed Dingiswayo. That the Black One will never forget. But Zwide is dead because of the Black One; it is his son Sikhunyana who now leads the Ndwandwe spears. The brother of Sikhunyana has told our Black One much and now the Ndwandwe tribe will be eaten up. I think we will go with the Black One when he goes to make his enemies eat the earth.'

And indeed the air was full of excitement and repressed violence. Warriors came to the royal kraal from all directions and commands were sent to the white men to come to Tshaka's support, which they did, even if reluctantly.

Pallidly the white men protested that they had no right to participate in a war without the sanction of their king; and Tshaka smiled with great gentleness and pointed out that in the land of the AmaZulu his was the power of rule and command; even in that portion of land which he had ceded to the white men all who continued in the land of the living did so by virtue of his clemency.

'Would your king,' Tshaka demanded, 'send avengers if *you* died?' and his smile suggested that kings had more important matters for their attention. 'It seems that these avengers would have great distances to come and what could a handful of white men do against my regiments? Despite their guns. That, at least, we will have from you seeing that you so ardently desire to support me. You may let Hlambamanzi have the use of that gun; after we have eaten our enemies it will be returned to you.'

The white men protested vehemently and Tshaka watched and listened, apparently much amused. Then, all at once, his smile became gentle indeed and he pointed a finger at Lieutenant Farewell, Fynn's companion, and said, 'Take his gun,' which order was instantly carried out by attendant warriors. 'Again I remind you that your lives depend on my clemency. It is my whim to have you for my friends, particularly Fynn. Do not trust a caprice. Earn friendship. Because of my affection for you, Fynn, I shall not require you to take part in any battle; I will also excuse the other white men. But you will give me your company.'

Thoroughly ruffled and shaken the white men retired to the quarters allocated to them; in the darkness of night Tshaka rose up with his men and set his feet upon the trails leading to the place where he intended overcoming Sikhunyana's forces; and in the morning the white men, guided by two Indunas, followed in Tshaka's footsteps, and found the king sixty miles away at Nobamba where had lived Tshaka's father, Senzangakhona.

Fynn, his dignity still shaken, listened to the praises being sung to Tshaka as regiments stamped off, and could not quite conceal his ironic reflections. The air was full of the thunder of male voices and the kraal black with people; yet it had to be admitted that all was precision and order; Tshaka had everything under rigid control and permitted no confusion anywhere.

After an interval of rest Tshaka continued the march: fifty thousand men, women and children, male and female regiments, women of the isigodlo, and small boys who acted as carriers to the warriors. The earth trembled and wild animals fled and a great cloud of moving dust filtered the hot rays of the sun. The march continued through the morning hours and surged through the scorching heat of noon and swept on until a scarlet sky ushered in a wild sunset; and now confusion came indeed, and a madness, for all were weary to the point of exhaustion and debased by a blind, animal craving for water; when a river was approached Tshaka and those regiments forming the first thrust of the spearhead stopped and drank and continued and left the little river muddy; and those that followed behaved like beasts, and men and particularly children died in the mad rush.

The moon was already riding high in the dark heavens when the impi came to a halt at a kraal whose people had in the past come under Tshaka's rule; not many of them were left for Tshaka had indeed eaten them, but they were well acquainted with the enemy country and for this reason engaged as spies and guides.

The following day the march continued, but in the morning Tshaka called for a rest and cattle were slaughtered and eaten, and a white man, Farewell, was injured by an ox. Tshaka gave instructions that Farewell was to remain, and with him were left Indunas who had the care of Tshaka's women.

Thola was amongst these women.

'But I want to go on,' she protested mutinously, despite her aching weariness. 'Why must I remain here?'

'The Black One wishes us to remain in safety,' a sister murmured complacently.

'I must speak to him,' Thola cried, agitation mounting. 'There must be some way I can get to him.'

'In times of war the Black One does not remember women,' the head of the seraglio said, and her word was absolute law for she was of royal blood. 'Be still now and rest.'

'People say the king is always at the forefront of the battle,' Thola said; she did not dare add, 'I am afraid for him.'

'Be still,' the woman commanded again.

But Thola could not be still. 'My God,' she thought, 'here I am clamouring for *his* safety. I am praying for *him.* A few days ago I was so sickened that I was glad because he did not send for me. Oh God, don't let anything happen to him. Let him live. Please let him *live.*'

She did not weep when Tshaka departed with his warriors: she followed the great cloud of dust with eyes that strained to pierce the enveloping obscurity of powdery, yellow sand; and her throat seemed as dry as that billowing dust, and it was agony to think 'If he should die – if *he* should die –'

The army fanned out and proceeded in a great line and again birds and animals fled before; at night the army encamped and rested in that spot for two days; and there was singing and dancing and countless camp-fires glowed redly upon black skins; and plumed head-dresses swayed and dipped.

When the march swept on again Fynn was directed to join a regiment at the forefront and became separated from Tshaka, and Fynn waited with this detachment in a great cave in a mountain. Tshaka came and the impi entered a forest and remained there, and scouts went out and plundered the countryside and returned with their booty, and amongst the gloom of the trees the people sat down and ate and the leaves of the trees sighed plaintively above them. And then they slept.

The regiments now took up their positions and they formed the horns of a bull; as the bull roared and charged, the horns would encircle.

On the side of a mountain the strength of Sikhun-yana waited; with their bodies the warriors formed a great circle around the wealth of the nation – the cattle – and behind them sat a great concourse of women and children, also protected by the living shield.

The men of the AmaZulu approached them, march-ing up close to them, and stood still; and the warriors of

Sikhunyana remained motionless; and the wind was hot with death.

Hlambamanzi fired his gun at the enemy, and the enemy spat their derision, but did not move; and he fired again, and then again; and suddenly there was screaming and wild cries of war, and the two forces leapt forward to meet, and assegais were hurled and short stabbing spears sank into flesh and were jerked out red with blood; and then a pause came in the violence; and with the second charge the AmaZulu were no longer men but screaming dealers of death; and at the third charge they were berserk, the smell of blood in their distended nostrils, and the hideous frenzy of death cries in their ears. With the enemy routed Tshaka's warriors slew the women and children and drove the enemy's cattle before them and occupied the kraal of Sikhunyana; and it had taken Tshaka no more than ninety minutes to destroy a nation; and of the forty thousand of that nation few were left. And chiefs commanded that the enemy wounded should be given the mercy of death.

Then the regiments of Tshaka brought out those who had shown cowardice and these men were put to death.

And the warriors were purified by the eating of a medicine root; and those who had killed added a sign in the shape of a piece of wood to a necklace which they had about their necks, and to this necklace they also added bits of the medicine root; and they went to a river and washed.

Now the time came to return victoriously home. Yet more battles took place against vassals of the defeated Sikhunyana; one force, headed by a chief by the name of Beje, managed to rout a regiment of the AmaZulu; and members of this regiment escaped and returned to Tshaka, and Tshaka was contemptuous of them as cowards who had shown their back to the enemy; and the cowards were killed.

And Tshaka left regiments to overcome Beje and turned his face towards his kraal.

And the white men left.

And later servants of the white men raped the daughter of a Zulu chief and Tshaka's rage was very great, but when he was assured that in the land of white men such a crime was considered just as heinous he did no harm to the white men.

He decided to attack Beje again – who had proved a difficult foe – and the white men, conscious of the misdeeds of their servants, gave him their support, and Beje was defeated.

And Tshaka went to another kraal, Dukuza, the place where one loses one's way.

Dukuza was set upon a hill and overlooked other rolling hills, and close by a river flowed down to the sea, which was not many miles distant and could be seen from high prominences. The countryside was covered by high, waving grasses, and fever trees cast their shadows upon the greenness; and the air was full of the tang of the sea and sultry and somnolent.

Tshaka stood on a high place and looked towards the blueness of the great water over which the white men had come to his land and his thoughts were troubled.

Even now Fynn was at his settlement at the bay where the great ridge of land humped itself against the sea; and with Fynn were thousands of black people who had found refuge in Fynn's protection: these were people who had fled from the might of the AmaZulu.

And he, the king of the black people, permitted this for he had affection for Fynn; and the fact that Fynn had many under him lent the white man an importance which he would not otherwise have possessed.

Beyond Fynn's settlement were mutinous tribes, and beyond these unconquered peoples, and beyond these the frontiers of the country which the white men had taken and occupied and made into a white stronghold.

Tshaka turned and looked towards the unknown fastness of Africa: behind him the sea; to his right the Tonga peoples, craven and subdued; then the Swazi, undefeated in their never-ending mountains; then somewhere in the unknown a nation Mzilikazi had forged, that recalcitrant and much-loved captain who had turned traitor and departed with many people, stealing like a thief; and Soshangana, another traitor, with the tribes he had bound together.

He was encircled by enemies whose brutality he understood and threatened by a white foe whose cunning he did not underestimate.

Yet neither cunning nor superior weapons of war would overcome the black holders of the land if all resisted as one man under one ruler.

The life of a man was short: the wind came and carried his breath away; a spear entered his flesh in battle and he was left behind; as year succeeded year a tiredness came to his limbs and a film of age obscured the keenness of his vision.

Neither death nor age would stand back for the objectification of an ideal.

He had to live; he had to live on and on in the prime of his vigour.

He was the bulwark of this land against all other lands.

His alone was the power to make of his people an unconquerable nation.

That he knew.

9

Now that Tshaka was not at Bulawayo the days seemed to Thola to be filled with a burning bitterness. It seemed so long ago that he had set out to make war on Sikhunyana; the day that she had prayed for his life had already become a dim memory, and the longing for his nearness wiped away all recollections of his immense cruelty.

She heard that he had left Dukuza and gone to Dibinhlanga, one of his other kraals, and was much occupied in hunting elephant; and then joyous tidings came that he was on his way to Bulawayo; and all sleepiness departed from the kraal and a febrile activity took its place. That look of tranquillity which descended when the king was absent was washed away from every face; everywhere were turmoil and expectancy, for no one was there mere existence now: every man, woman and child *lived*.

Across the hills he came, splendid and victorious, he and his warriors, chanting as they strode through deep valleys and up boulder-strewn slopes; and the people went out to meet him, the women singing and dancing; and his eyes looked for and found Thola and a great weakness invaded her.

He had travelled far and yet he was not weary and neither were his captains and their regiments; tremendous dances took place, and heroic choruses, and the warriors giya'd – mimed their powerful deeds of war – and all sang Tshaka's Praise Songs. Many cattle were slaughtered and great feasting followed and the dogs had a great day licking clean the meat platters; and the cockroaches, those scavengers, came down from the walls of the huts in their thousands and fulfilled the task for which they were kept and swept bare every utensil of every morsel of food; and staggered, gorged, back to their safe retreats.

Because he sent for others and not for her she was bitter against him and said to UmuSa, 'I suppose now death will come again. This is not the land of heaven: this is the kingdom of murder and death. I longed to find this magnificent king of whom I had heard and I encountered many dangers to come to him – and I found a madman!'

UmuSa moved away, carefully looking around, but the hut was empty. Thola became impatient with her and reflected that she was, after all, an ignorant savage, accustomed to vile and sudden death, and probably not over-shocked. But if UmuSa knew nothing of civilisation and believed the moon was a platter in the sky and never doubted the power of witchcraft or spirit manifestations, nevertheless she had her own wisdom.

'Is there no death in the country from which you come?' she asked. 'Do all men live until their age is so great that they are sent to the land of the spirits because life has become a burden to them? It is so then?'

'It is not so,' Thola admitted, taken aback.

'And if we loved our lord in his magnificence, shall we love him less when his judgment demands death?'

'Love,' Thola said, thinking of the fat, silly, bovine women now in Tshaka's company 'do not speak of love to me. At least I shall no longer be troubled. Tshaka has forgotten me.' She spat his name defiantly and UmuSa trembled.

'Do not believe that. You will see him soon.'

'He did not send for me.'

'Soon he will send for you.'

'You think that I do not know that you are in peril. I know that you are going to have a child and I know what that means. I have seen Tshaka's women drinking bad medicine because they conceived and were desperate to rid their bodies of fruit which would cost them their lives. Oh God, that is what I do not understand. He is the one responsible for the quickening. He knows what pregnancy will bring; why does he not leave women alone – altogether?'

'Which of us,' UmuSa said reasonably, 'would wish to be left alone? We are all happy to be taken to him. There is not a woman here who would leave if she could; even those who have never been with him live in the hope that he will beckon. Is there a woman in the land who would refuse him?'

Thola closed her eyes and shuddered and thought 'No, not even I. I would go to him now.'

'Even you,' UmuSa murmured, 'even you who are so defiant and challenge death every time your tongue moves. Even if he were just a warrior and not a king it would still be so. My friend,' and her eyes were bright with compassion, 'be careful when next you speak to the Elephant. Do not try him too far.'

'I think I would be glad to die.'

'But we will be desolate.'

Deeply touched Thola returned to UmuSa's pregnancy. 'You have not taken medicine. Perhaps you tried to rid yourself of the child while I was away at the kraal where the white man lay ill. Did you?'

UmuSa shook her head.

'Are you not afraid?'

'I am afraid. But I have always longed for a child. In the black hours of night my cheeks have been wet with tears because it seemed that I was barren. I did not dare ask a doctor for help, but always I hoped.'

'But the child will die!'

'That I know but I cannot believe. Somehow I dream that my son lives in favour with the king. Who knows? Life may remain.'

Thola rubbed her chin, unconsciously imitating Tshaka's action when he was in a meditative mood. 'Perhaps there is a way. Perhaps we can think of something. We might be able to send the child away – or get you away.'

UmuSa waited dumbly.

'We must plan and scheme.'

Two, three, four, five days passed, and when the fear that Tshaka had indeed forgotten her turned her into a raging demon, suddenly she was summoned; and she found him aged; a white hair or two and a drawn furrow about his lips and a restlessness he had not shown before.

'Come, sit here,' he commanded her, and she sat at his knees and looked up at him, her eyes searching out the furrows in his face. 'You will be glad to hear that the lad who came here with you is shaping well. His spear has tasted blood and is ever hungry. He took part in a small skirmish. A small skirmish when so many enemies crouch and wait. It chafes me. It chafes me!'

'My father,' Thola murmured, bending her head.

'Malanga,' Tshaka said, 'that is his name, is it not?' and his eyes swivelled around and fastened on her. 'The lad you love so well. The child who stood against one of my regiments for your sake. You are thin, flower of maturity.'

'I grieved for you, Lord.'

'But you had a haughty air about you, I am told.'

'It is my way, Lord. When I am most desolate a look of pride comes.'

'Let it not come in my presence. You do not wear the rings I gave you,' and his finger touched her throat.

'I leave my throat free for the touch of your hands, Lord. What are ornaments compared to that?'

'You do not wear my gifts because you fear your neck will become sore,' Tshaka countered, and a jarring note in his voice alerted her. 'Do you know that when a warrior has dipped his assegai in blood he must be cleansed? There are ways of purifying those who spill blood and take a life. I have in mind that you shall purify the lad – this lad – you love so well.'

'I will send for the medicine,' Thola said, shivering at his voice.

'Also the warrior must know a woman. You will go to Malanga!'

Her head jerked up, unbelief on her face, but the oriental eyes were hard and the expression on the strong face inscrutable; she forgot that she was in the presence of the king and gripped his knees and cradled her head on him and cried, 'Ah, no!' her voice cracking on a high note, and her heart rebelled with pain that he loved her so little when she worshipped him.

'No one disobeys my command,' Tshaka said, the jarring note again distorting his voice.

'Kill me then, Lord,' Thola pleaded, and her fingers tightened on their feverish clasp, and Tshaka remained unyielding. 'I belong to *you*.'

'Of what use is it to belong where you are not wanted? Go where you are bidden and do what you are directed so that you may live.'

'I would rather die . . .'

'Once before I told you that death is easy but the way of death is hard.'

'I will die any death. Any death.'

'In fire?' he asked, and Thola began to weep.

'In fire,' she said, 'even in fire.'

'I am no longer a man,' Tshaka muttered and groaned deeply. 'A woman even defies me. I think you shall die slowly as did the woman for whom Fynn pleaded. Or perhaps you would wish to be caged with a wild animal or given to the crocodiles? Or be planted upon a sharp stick as a fruit spiked upon a thin branch?'

She rubbed her cheeks against his knees and her warm tears fell upon them and she could not speak.

'Thola,' the deep voice said, and again, 'Thola,' and she looked up and there were tears in the king's eyes, and she sighed his name, and he said, 'Ah, Thola,' and lifted her up to him in one swift movement.

But even then his caresses were brief and too soon he directed her to return to her quarters and the demon raged again in her when his servant called out the names of women and they departed slyly to wait upon the king's pleasure.

But it became obvious to her that she had incurred the king's anger; very seldom did he send for her and even those royal moments were short; always she was sent back to her quarters while others remained through the hours of the night with him.

And Thola turned to UmuSa, whose time was near at hand, for comfort. UmuSa was by now living in virtual seclusion; pathetically she followed all the rules governing a pregnant woman and abstained from the various taboos, just as if her child would indeed live. Thola had thought herself into a state of near-madness but could find no way to save the child. Once she had considered asking Malanga for help but UmuSa had warned her against having anything to do with the boy. Tshaka was most determined that his women should be faithful; on the suspicion that a girl in one of his seraglios had misbehaved with a warrior, the warrior and the entire regiment to which he belonged had been executed and the entire seraglio slaughtered. Throughout the kingdom, of course, the penalty for adultery was death, but at that time many innocents had died.

'Are all the people of this country so cruel?' Thola asked wanly.

'Many are far worse than our lord,' UmuSa replied. 'Compare the Black One to the rulers of other peoples and he is as gentle as a calf. They torture because they delight in witnessing suffering: he does not. They kill for the sake of killing: the Black One always kills for a purpose.'

'And then what does his cruelty matter? I am such a hypocrite, UmuSa. I shudder and yet I long for him. I also have tears upon my cheeks every night. He seldom sends for me and when he does I remain with him for so short a space – and then he speaks to me – nothing more.'

She could not even pray for UmuSa: somehow, the fact that she lived in Tshaka's kraal and *loved* him removed her too far from grace; left upon her an imprint of darkness which obscured God's light. So must an excommunicated one feel, she thought. Yet, with all that care and fear, she bloomed as she had never bloomed before. A sheen and a lustre softened her skin, grace dwelt in her movements, and a warmness in her eyes and smile drew admiration. With her admission to herself that Tshaka ruled her completely and that her life was a waiting to be summoned to him, a certain peace had come: she loved a savage forever and always and her feet would never stray from the path upon which she had set them. Tshaka alone mattered.

'If only I could help you,' she nevertheless murmured to UmuSa, and the woman shook her head and sighed.

'No one can help me. I will hear my child cry – once perhaps – and then he will be strangled – and I want to die with him. I will go with him into the land of the spirits and there I will be a mother and he a child. He will have no father for the Black One will not acknowledge him. You must leave me now, my sister, so that you may not become unclean. Should the Black One send for you you will not be able to go to him if you have been with me.' She loosened the covering which she had worn across her breasts during her pregnancy. 'The child will soon be here.'

Old women came to deliver the baby, but in secrecy, so that Tshaka might not be troubled at the thought that a child had been born of his strength 'There is one thing for which I wish,' UmuSa whispered, and Thola hesitated at the opening to the hut and then returned to the labouring woman. 'I have wished for a little oil from the body of the father of the child – a scraping from that place where contact from the earth might have left a few grains of dust upon him – dust might have settled on his arms or in the palms of his hands. Such dust – a little dust – to give the child – quickly – before he is strangled. For a living child it is great medicine and places in its body the virtues of its clan. I would wish my child to take that medicine with him when he goes into the land of spirits. But this is not possible.'

'You have been wicked,' one old midwife announced. 'You will have a difficult birth. You have eaten your meals on your feet and thus the child is standing on his feet and his feet will enter the world first. If the father could come and perform the necessary ceremony with you, the birth will be easier. But he will not come.'

'The child has no father,' UmuSa said and buried her face in her hands and wept.

Now Thola jeopardised her life for the sake of UmuSa and in doing so she unintentionally sentenced to death many people. She humbly requested a private audience of Tshaka, saying the matter was of utmost importance and that she had to speak to him; and this he granted, with impatience, and was not the lover when she crept into his royal hut. In the mornings he sometimes rested for a while and lately he had been having dreams that disturbed his sleep; and he was weary that day and frowned on her.

But, with her bloom upon her, she was very lovely to look at, and she knew this and made the most of her beauty; and Tshaka found her mind of great attraction too and this caused him to deal mercifully with her; and when she saw the softening of his features she ventured close to him, on her knees, and he did not reprove her.

'What is it? You have taken me off my sleeping-mat,' he said to her, not querulously, but as if in surprise that a woman could so disturb him.

'Lord, in the hours of the night I had a dream about you which has filled me with concern ever since.'

The sleepiness vanished from his face and his eyes daunted her with the intensity of their stare.

'May I see your hands, Lord?' she asked, and stilled the trembling starting within her; and, after a moment's hesitation, Tshaka held out his hands; as she took them she was careful to let her nails scrape gently along his skin; and then she turned his hands over and examined the palms and poked beneath his finger nails, and sighed as if in great relief.

'What did you dream?' he asked.

'I had a dream that a wound had been inflicted beneath one of your nails and that it was starting to fester and that it would infect all your body,' Thola muttered, 'and I was greatly distressed for, although it was but a dream, anything that could be of harm to my lord causes me infinite concern.'

'I have often told you that you are a very forward woman,' Tshaka said sombrely, 'but you are also a wise woman. When you first came to me it was said that your mother was a witch who roamed the hills. We live in this world but we must concede that there is another whence our shadows go when we die; and certainly much wisdom is in that world: all the wisdom of our forefathers. And in speaking to you I have discovered that you are different from all other women.

You think as a man and sometimes more than a man. Therefore I often listen to you where another would not live to say the things you say; and I set store by the words of your mouth. But let your concern ever be for me and not against me.'

'Lord,' Thola said, speaking from her heart, 'no one has ever loved as I love you.'

'Undoubtedly for which reason you feel it right to criticise me whenever possible,' Tshaka observed dryly. 'I trust you, my flower. I do not have to ask for love or obedience; that I can command, and it pleases me to trust you.'

'One cannot command love,' Thola put in, greatly daring. 'Think, Lord. Can the heart be commanded to love? Is it not that the people love you for yourself? For your beauty and power and wisdom?'

'Is it?' he said, still sombre.

'That is why I love you. Others may fear, not love. It seems to me that you are too much feared.'

'A dog understands strength; if a lion treated a buck with kindness, the gentle buck might bore the lion with his horns and kill the most powerful of beasts. My dogs understand strength.'

'A man is more than a dog.'

'Therefore a man needs even greater control. We will see what your dream portends, flower of maturity. Leave me now.'

Thola crept out and sped to her hut and scraped carefully beneath her fingers and made a little mud pellet and hastened to UmuSa and quickly pressed the tiny pellet into the palm of UmuSa's hand and whispered in her ear, and then escaped and went about her business with a palpitating heart. She had tampered with the king's person and all that he was and all that belonged to his body was sacred.

And when the child was born men came to strangle

it; the mother heard its cry and clasped it and held it to her breast and would not let it go; the men struggled with her, tearing at the child, and she evaded them and ran screaming out of the hut, towards Tshaka, and the people stood in amazement; and Tshaka, tall and arrogant, watched her progress, and called a warrior, and a vein in his forehead began to throb. The warrior stopped UmuSa's headlong flight and Tshaka gripped the child; his face became terrible and in his eyes there was a look of intolerable suffering; and he dashed the child hard on the ground and it was dead.

The woman, who at first had seemed about to attack the king, fell on her knees, and her eyeballs swivelled this way and that; and her breathing was hoarse; and she could not bend her head because of the soreness, although the brass rings had long since been removed from her neck.

Tshaka said one word, 'Kill!' and men took UmuSa away; and she went submissively, as if her soul had already joined her child and only the husk, her body, moved the way it was dragged.

Now a cleansing took place. The king was given strengthening medicines by the doctors: first a black medicine which was very potent, followed by a white medicine to make him vomit up the black medicine; and this he did, copiously. And gall bladders were torn out of living calves and the gall sprinkled on the king; and there was much fear in the kraal; and the women belonging to the king went about with careful softness and spoke no words.

The hut where UmuSa lived was cleansed: it was swept and new manure placed upon the floor, and a fire was made so that the smoke from the fire billowed around and filled the hut; and warriors were despatched to the distant home of UmuSa and her father and mother died and all her family; and their dwellings were left to fall to rubble beneath the power of the wind and the rain.

And three more women died in Tshaka's kraal, one because of the results of a medicine she had taken to remove the fruit in her womb.

Thola did not see Tshaka for some time for he went off, in the midst of a regiment, to visit some other military kraal. When he returned the white men came, which put him in a good temper. There was much dancing and feasting and a review of the royal herd, and a great hunt was planned. Thola had so often been told of Tshaka's fearlessness that she was afraid that he might endanger his life and she waited anxiously for the end of the hunt; and when he came back to the kraal she had been right to fear for him. Tshaka had very nearly been savaged by a ravening lion; indeed several of his warriors had died because they had interposed their bodies between the lion and the king. The warriors had lived long enough to see the wild beast slain, for Tshaka had leaped at it and driven his short assegai into its heart, and with their last breath they had applauded their king's wild courage. Tshaka sorrowed over the death of these brave men and sent their families many cattle; and he was additionally depressed by the fact that one shot from the white man's gun had stopped a huge bull elephant. Up till that moment he had convinced himself that no white army could stand against the pride of his impis. He commanded his people again to show white men every respect; he directed his dogs to bow to the superior knowledge of the white men and to treat them as fathers; and when the white men left he talked this over with Thola.

'Lord,' she reminded him, 'perhaps all those with white skins are not good as these men are good. If you command your people to bow before them the people may give way to rogues and thieves and murderers.'

'That I know,' Tshaka admitted heavily. His chin was sunk on his chest and melancholia weighed him down. 'I must be the bulwark against the white men who are evil. I think that when I go they will come and eat up the land and leave my people without a country. They will turn my warriors into servants, for against their knowledge my bravest and best are as children. This I have seen. My great chiefs will run to do their bidding and their wives cook their food. The people of heaven will become slaves.'

'Not slaves, Lord. Such proud people can never be slaves.'

'We trade with white people who live towards the east near the sea. There those who are black are proud too, and already they are slaves. I have no mercy on slavers.' He took snuff and stared before him and Thola could not determine his thoughts for his mind had escaped her. She longed to comfort him and did not know how. He was not a man who could find solace in the arts of love; no hunger of the senses could distract him.

'Lord,' she murmured at last, 'you are still young and strong. The country is secure, so secure in the mighty palms of your hands. North, south, east and west you have conquered and no one mutters against you. Let not gloomy thoughts cast you down.'

'Young,' he repeated and his hand went up to his chin. 'So young that I am near to becoming a grey-beard. You see even Fynn, this white man whom I protect and love, even he denies me the secret of youth. Again and again I have asked for this oil which staves off greyness, and never has he provided it, despite all the elephant tusks I place at his disposal. It must be that his king – this UmGeorge – reserves it for his own use. I did not like to see the power of the white man's gun. I was not happy when the bull elephant fell. I must keep my army active, flower of maturity. I must keep my country strong and ready – my warriors poised to run into battle at the blink of an eyelid.'

She had wanted to speak to him about UmuSa; the memory of UmuSa's death and the fate of the child lay like a shadow upon every day. But how could she trespass upon his present concern and how could she say that gentleness and kindness would overcome his difficulties? He knew that gentleness and kindness would lose him his power, and when his power went the speedy deterioration of his country would set in, and the people of heaven would return to obscurity. Nevertheless, she tried.

'Lord,' she said, 'you rule by power. Often I have asked you whether you kill for the sake of killing.'

'Who would wish to kill for the sake of killing?' he demanded impatiently. 'Men are like hyenas: they never venture near the strong. Men are also like children: let them once disobey and their disobedience will increase. If I show weakness how long will my enemies hold back? Will they understand kindness? Will they, flower of maturity?'

'But the women, Lord. And the children.'

'Women can be a great source of trouble. They can put devious thoughts into the hearts of their men and into the hearts of their children. To conquer one must destroy and to remain the conqueror one must continue destroying.' He sent her an oblique glance. 'Do you imagine it is easy to order the death of a child – a woman – a man? Dadewet-u! It is easier to attack a crocodile and kill him with bare hands.'

'Ah, Lord,' Thola whispered, responding to the suffering in him, and involuntarily her hands went out to him, but he ignored her.

'Do you not understand that to make a nation people must act and live as a unit? But for me the people would still be isolated tribal pockets with different allegiances, torn with stupid warfare. I have welded these tribes into a whole and soon I will subjugate and absorb even those in lands now unknown to me: all black tribes across the great rivers. I will set my feet upon the plains, the mountains and the valleys and the people of heaven will own the land from sea to sea.' His long fingers rubbed at his chin and his brows furrowed. 'If I have the time. If I have the time, flower of maturity. Now and again that darkness descends and I feel . . .' he paused and sighed. 'When power has been consolidated then we can speak of peace and kindness; then young men may marry and scatter their strength in the making of children and the enjoying of wives. But not yet. Not yet.'

Moodily he rested his chin on his hand and stared into the flames shooting from the fire at the far end of the hut.

'Those who come out of the sea – they are a danger to my people.'

In comparison to the white men, Thola thought, how like a child you are: you are like an immensely clever child; and you are, on occasion, as naïve as a child, but your brilliant childishness is merciless; you have the cruelty of a child, you and all your people. When necessary you slaughter with total abandon; at other times you are as tender as a mother with her baby. Yet, in your own self, there is a greatness of adult wisdom too. And genius. You are a complete paradox.

'I must have this youth-giving oil,' Tshaka said, returning to his preoccupation with eternal vigour. 'It must be that Fynn, whom I have made my friend, would rather have me living as a spirit with the spirits of my fathers than alive and potent in the land of the AmaZulu.'

Thola could not find it in her heart to ridicule him

for his beliefs. The Zulu concept of creation and after-life — what superiority did her own concepts have? What were the spirits of the fathers but intermediaries between man and God? God — that omnipotent and mysterious principle behind all manifestation, so remote that the Zulu mind did not dwell too much upon deity. How could she scoff at a creator sprung from a bed of reeds when all she had to offer were a man, his rib, fig leaves and apples? Which tenet was the droller? Again solace came to her in the thought that for the AmaZulu there was no such thing as sin: acts committed against the welfare of the tribe and the direct intercessor, the king, were wrong, but no man wept because of acts of commission and omission. No man was hounded into a life of spurious rectitude through fear of torture in hell; he ordered his way because of his sense of responsibility; he was saner and healthier in mind than those obsessively heedful of a morbid goodness, a distortion of meekness and humbleness. He did not dwell in long introspection of his sins, those ugly, dirty, little habits that grow in darkness and bring to mind the sickly whiteness of plants sprouting in some dank place far from the light of the sun. He did not live in an unnatural, constrained world in order to save his frightened little soul from the fires of hell; he was not noxious in the sight of God, that strange God of the white men who breathed vengeance one moment and tenderly spoke dulcet words of love the next moment.

She thought of Jesus: ah, He was a mighty fighter, with strength in Him; He was not given to womanly seizures and soul searchings; when He wept it was in sorrow for others; power and purpose were in His every act. And a strong and mighty soul John must have been, and Mark and Luke and Matthew; all, all the other disciples too, men of shining splendour. Always they were concerned for others.

Tshaka moved and she jumped; he tilted her chin and studied her face intently.

'You have deep thoughts, flower of maturity. You have the body of a woman and the mind of a man and you can sit in quietness and bring benison with your presence.'

Unconsciously she drew nearer to him.

'When I was a child,' he continued, 'I did not see it that way, but my mother had those qualities too. She was always ready to protect me and because of me her life was hard. I was much mocked by others and made to bear a great deal of pain; and because I was mocked I became hard in my determination and the very ones who injured me taught me to be strong and to take what I wanted. I proved my bravery when Dingiswayo was king: I became the hero of his army and justified the words of those who said I had courage; and my war cry was "Sigidi" – I was the slayer of thousands. I killed a giant for Dingiswayo, a madman who dwelt safely on high ground. No one dared challenge him but I attacked and killed him; and I slaughtered Dingiswayo's enemies and ate up all who stood against him; I looked to him as a father and it was great sorrow when, in the end, treachery brought him death. I took his tribe and made them one with the people of heaven – the people of my father. I have achieved great things,' and his voice was flat and matter-of-fact.

'You do not know how great,' Thola murmured, and wished he would lift her face again.

'It is said that I am descended from a white ancestor,' Tshaka said suddenly and began to shake with unexpected laughter. 'Do you think so, flower of maturity?'

'You are the great Black One,' Thola replied, smiling with him.

'That I am. No doubt' – and a faint irony tinged his words – 'these white men would give all they possess to

126

have a black skin. Go now, my flower. I have much to ponder.'

'Lord,' she said hurriedly, 'let me just ask – Lord, these days you no longer regard me. You speak with me – indeed – but others comfort you in the hours of sleep – then you do not want me . . .'

'You speak truly,' and he turned his head away from her.

'You do not want me at all,' and she bent her head; and he put out a hand to touch her, hesitated and drew back, and the silence lengthened and grew heavy.

'I will have your mind,' he said at last; then in an undertone, 'I will keep you in safety always.'

10

THOLA watched the making of shields, work for the men of the regiments, and then word went out that a beast was to be chosen for a new shield for the king. About a dozen white oxen were herded together and then the beasts were allowed to spread out a little and careful examinations were made to discover some flaw in the animals and the imperfect ones were driven away. Men stood around laughing and gesticulating and an air of pleasurable excitement pervaded the kraal. Tshaka walked around the beasts, eyeing them narrowly, and listened to comments which came from all sides. One of his Indunas, a big, fat man, made some ribald remark and a shout of male laughter startled the birds wheeling overhead.

'This one,' a captain of a regiment cried and pointed to a great white ox and Tshaka smiled and made a disclaiming gesture, and his long hands moved in a graceful arc as if in imitation of the curving wings of a bird.

'This one,' he said and pointed to a smaller animal which stood compact and square. 'The others move around too much; they do not conserve energy.'

With sycophantic eagerness many applauded his choice and he glanced at them impatiently and contemptuously.

'You,' said Tshaka to the captain, 'will increase my herds by twenty cattle if I am right; if you are right I will swell the numbers of your herd by thirty,' and a eulogistic murmur rose from the people massed around.

Of all gathered there he was the most simply dressed; indeed Thola had noticed in the past that it was only in his war attire that he was ornamented with massive decorations of beads and other finery; yet he stood out amongst his warriors now and his personal magnificence dimmed the splendour of their adornments.

Sharply he gave an order and men ran forward: so many that their forms milled around the oxen and obscured vision; and there was a great bellowing and the bellowing became a whimpering; the desolate sound a very small animal coughs out when it is near death and in very acute pain.

And Thola saw that the cattle had been flayed alive and that they had been left to die in a hideous torment, a burning agony that seared every raw and bleeding inch of their bodies; and one by one they died, and the beast Tshaka had chosen was the last to fall upon its knees.

A great shout echoed over the royal kraal; and then came delighted laughter and the hide of this ox was carried away in triumph.

Thola's hands flew to her mouth and a retching shudder jerked her body and when she looked up again she found the king's burning eyes focused upon her; and the outlines of his features wavered so that it seemed as if she were looking at him through water; and the distortion increased and she turned away and gulped air into her lungs and tried to steady herself.

In the women's quarters there was no one to whom she could turn; UmuSa alone had given the hand of friendship; the other women she knew, instinctively, she could not trust. Yet when a tall woman, the sister of Umbopha, an Induna of the king, made sullen overtures, Thola could not help responding. While she had been the king's favourite she had not been aware of loneliness but now that she was with Tshaka only occasionally the nights were always empty and often the days as well.

'You could not retain your food this morning,' the woman said and her eyes darted maliciously at Thola's flat stomach. 'That is strange for we know that you have not been with the king for many months – and our guards are so ugly.'

'If you mean that I am with child . . .' Thola began indignantly.

'Are you?' the woman whispered silkily.

'I am as I was when I first came to live here.'

'That is sad for you. At first it appeared as if the Black One had singled you out. Perhaps you wearied him with too many words of love.'

Thola looked up questioningly.

'We see how you love the king. When he calls for you you go to him as if apparelled in light.' The woman laughed shrilly. 'Many, many years ago the Black One loved a woman; but she became an obstacle in his way and he killed her with his own hands.' The shrill laughter with the threatening nuance came again. 'If you repeat my words to the king I too will die.' With studied nonchalance she worked her fingers underneath the beads of her arm-band and twisted the bright ring around and around. 'But I have no fear for you are a coward about death. You vomit over the death of an animal.'

'I am a coward,' Thola agreed; and the recollection of the choosing of the shield was so vivid that her stomach knotted in rebellion again and her anger against the woman was dissipated.

'The Black One has use for you only for the words of your mouth,' the woman taunted. 'Perhaps you are too thin,' and she glanced complacently at the plumpness of her shining arms.

Thola left her abruptly but the barbed words remained to prick her and when she was again taken into Tshaka's presence determination had coalesced within her and she was intent on discovering his true feelings.

As always he motioned for the other women to remain in the shadows at the far end of the hut and their soft singing lulled her; and heedless of danger she said, 'Lord, I think I must leave.'

'Indeed?' Tshaka said; his lazy posture did not change but she sensed a sudden alertness in him.

'For you do not want me.'

'Who has said so?'

'You, Lord. Not so much in words – but in actions. You prefer those silly, *fat* girls to me.'

The slightest glimmer of a smile disturbed his lips.

'In a little while you will command me to go and others will take my place.'

'No one takes your place, small one,' the king said. 'You have a mind of such sharp brightness. Is it possible that you do not yet understand?'

'What is there for me to understand?' Thola asked petulantly, aware that she was again falling under the spell of his voice and that she would leave without an answer unless she steeled herself.

'That I love you too deeply – courage in you which I sensed – and I was not mistaken – and your mind – which constantly affords me pleasure – and your beauty. You are beautiful.'

And now she was scarcely able to resist the mesmeric quality of his tones.

'But you do send me away,' she insisted. 'You send me away.'

'What is it you want from me?' he asked. 'That I should endanger your life? These others' – and he gestured towards the shadowed part of the hut where the women chanted so softly – 'mean nothing to me. They serve a purpose.'

'You are in a most gentle mood,' Thola said suddenly, quite side-tracked, and the laughter wrinkles around the king's oriental eyes deepened; emboldened she took his hand and brought it up to her face and held it against her cheek; after a short moment he drew back.

'You have not forgotten a woman whom you loved and who died – the child also died,' Tshaka said, harshness replacing his laughter.

'You said no harm need come to me,' Thola whispered, staring up at him pleadingly. 'You said I would not ever have to have a child.'

'With others,' the deep voice said, 'the choice is mine.'

The sudden leap in her heartbeats was almost a pain.

'If there is so much love,' she whispered, so low, so low she did not know if he would hear, 'then let me be your wife. Would my children be so great a danger to you?'

Almost terror came that she had dared too greatly; the shadows loomed around her as the flames licked about in the fire and Tshaka's shadow was grotesque against the walls of the hut.

'I will reveal to you all that is in my head and my heart,' the king said and sighed. 'I trust you, flower of maturity. There are many I can trust implicitly – those who love me and are loyal to me. I believe you are also completely loyal. When you came to me I did not question you closely. When one has suffered one can read the suffering in the eyes of another and it seemed to me that your life had been a sadness.'

'A sadness, Lord,' she said.

'Also it seemed to me that you were not one of our people: the ways of the white men were discovered in you. Such things belonged to the past; I left them in the past. Perhaps I am more perceptive than you supposed?'

She could only bend her head.

'I did not even question the lad who came with you.

You look at me with the same expression that is to be found in the eyes of the white men. Awe certainly, for I can destroy in an instant, but always superiority is present as well: the vastness of the knowledge which the white men possess and which makes me appear, at times, as a child. I am ignorant of all that knowledge; they bring me articles of clothing which give the impression that magic was used in their fashioning. And many products. Toys, Thola. Toys. Of what use are they in our way of life?' He paused and Thola did not have the courage to break the silence. 'Do not underestimate me as the white men underestimate me. There are many exceptions, yet I must say that my people are truly children; they are indeed children against the knowledge and might of the white men. But I am not a child, my flower. Tshaka is not a child.'

'My father,' she murmured.

'Again and again I have told you that I am the shield of my people. Once I spoke of slavery and without your realising it you disclosed your secret. You have been a slave.'

'I have been a slave, Lord,' she concurred and shuddered.

'And you wish *that* upon my people!' the deep, bass voice thundered; the singing stopped in little screams and at the far end of the hut the women crouched in abject terror. But when the king spoke again his voice was scarcely audible and very gentle. 'No, flower of maturity. I think you know I am a lonely man. That I have accepted. It is a price to be paid for what I have set myself to accomplish. Not even for you will my people suffer. Not even for you.'

'Some do not die,' Thola said stubbornly. 'The children die but the women live.' She clasped her hands and added urgently, 'If you are so mindful of your people why do you allow . . . allow . . . ?'

'Who would believe,' the king said, 'that Tshaka sits here defending his actions? With all your cleverness you have missed much. You have been with me for some time, my flower, and so few in the isigodlo have died. If I had no care for the women do you think only such a few would have died?'

She thought of the women who came to his sleeping-mat and shook her head in wonderment.

'I cannot afford that whispers should go about suggesting that the king is without potency; therefore children are born. But not many. I choose the women with great care; not the stupid ones; never those who have not the courage to accept the consequences. I seek out those who seek such fulfilment despite what it brings to them.'

'UmuSa did not have that courage,' Thola said quickly.

'She did indeed have that courage. You have your own kind of courage, my dear one, but not the courage to accept that your child will be destroyed.'

'Perhaps it is not courage. Perhaps it is lack of feeling,' Thola said and wept.

'That may be. We will not speak of this again.'

'Lord,' she whispered, lifting her head, 'just once – just once hold me near to you,' and she looked up into his face, at the autocratic lines of his lips and the granite set of his chin; and his eyes were inscrutable and she accepted defeat.

'Not – for – one small – moment?' she said stumblingly; and he touched her chin with great tenderness; and he sent her away and the other women as well. For many weeks no one from the isigodlo was taken into his hut.

11

SHE did not see the king, yet her heart sang; she yearned for his nearness, but there was no desolation for the knowledge that he loved her brought a glow of happiness that filled each day with impossible dreams. And she held herself proudly in the isigodlo and defied anyone to taunt her; the women, so many now neglected, lowered their eyes and avoided her.

Once she passed one of the old women who had delivered UmuSa and, in her glow of happiness, thought nothing of the sly glances sent her.

His desire for Macassar oil spurred Tshaka on to great hunting ventures and he went off with his warriors in search of elephant; during the expedition he met up with Fynn and Tshaka remembered that he wished to rebuild a kraal at some distance from Bulawayo and constrained Fynn to accompany him; and he passed Bulawayo by and also the kraal of Nandi, his mother, which was not far from Bulawayo; and when he arrived at the place where the kraal was to be erected messengers brought news that Nandi, whose name meant sweetness, was ill. And Tshaka was greatly troubled and sent doctors to her, and medicine he had obtained from Fynn; and he called his warriors together and returned in the direction of Bulawayo, his mind set upon reaching Nandi's kraal with utmost swiftness. Again and again runners approached and sorrowfully told the king that his mother was no better; throughout the night he marched; through the dark hours his feet bruised the grass and where the earth was desolate of greenness dust was raised to glow like silver mist in the faint moonlight. He kept his face turned towards the home of his mother; and he maintained a steady, even, tireless pace; and no man knew his thoughts. The feather above his head swayed and dipped in a never-changing rhythm; and he spoke no words.

When the dawn was still two hours distant he came to Bulawayo and he paused in his kraal and sent the white man, Fynn, to the home of Nandi; and he waited for news in silence. Fynn came to him and said that Nandi would surely die. He looked at the white man and listened to his words and his face was like a mask.

'Return again to my mother,' Tshaka said to the white man, 'whose name is sweetness.'

He sent his warriors away from him, but motioned to the greybeards to remain; and he sat through wan hours, staring at the ground before him; in absolute silence he kept this vigil; not even a sigh escaped him.

Men came softly to him and told him that Nandi was dead. He bent his head towards their words; then he stood up and said, 'Get ready as if for war,' and he went into his hut.

In the isígodlo the women waited fearfully; for them the night hours had passed on slow wings and they did not greet the morning star, iKhwezi, with jubilation, when it placed its brilliance in the sky; and when iLanga, the sun, appeared in the east and cast broad streamers of gold in the mist-blue, cloud-dappled sky they received no comfort from its warmth.

And Tshaka came out of his hut and he was dressed for war, and the women approached him; and the warriors, the captains, the chiefs, and the ordinary people. To all tidings were given of Nandi's death and people pulled off their decorative finery and bright beads fell upon the ground.

Nandi's son stood, his head resting upon the hand that held his assegai upright; and his tears fell upon the whiteness of his great shield. He made no sound and the people were silent with him. Tears sped down black faces; it seemed as if the sighing wind mourned; it seemed as if thick clouds dimmed the heavens. The minutes lengthened: five, ten, fifteen minutes passed; and the tears coursed down Tshaka's cheeks and his chest heaved; twenty minutes, and he pulled his head up and moaned, 'Maye ngo Mama. Ah, my mother!' and he gave a great cry, and cry after cry was jerked out of him, deep down from his throat, so that it seemed he would die of sorrow – that his deep sighs and wild cries were wrenching his life out of him.

The people began shrieking with him until the land echoed with shouts of grief and pain; and even little children joined in the suffering.

'Let all mourn,' an Induna screamed, flecks of foam appearing at the corners of his mouth; Tshaka looked at him and the king's eyes seemed to start from his head and his lips curved back from his teeth. 'Let all mourn for the mother of heaven,' the Induna cried.

The sister of Umbopha, who was standing beside Thola, said to another woman, 'Weep. Weep,' and her voice was urgent; deliberately she pushed a finger into her eyes and hurt herself. 'Weep, my sister.'

There were no tears in Thola. How could she weep for someone she hardly knew? How could she weep over the savage who was wailing like a woman; this Tshaka Zulu whom she worshipped yet for whom, at this moment, she felt only acute loathing; this man who terrified her and distorted her emotions and always bent her to his unpredictable will? Sudden distaste for him inundated her, and a repugnance for his uninhibited frenzy.

One woman, kinder than the rest, dashed her fingers

into Thola's eyes. Tears sprang out because of the stinging pain; and then Thola was able to weep; she wept because life was so much sorrow; she wept for the black king, yet confusedly she thought 'Satan! Whether devil or saint, suffer. Feel the sorrow you have given others. You are not above pain after all. You are not proof against the rake of grief,' and then she gasped and caught her breath, 'If you can love as much as this – if this is how you love!' and was ashamed that even now, torn by conflicting emotions, exultation could come because that was how she – perhaps – was loved by him.

The women wailed shrilly, weeping with great sobs; men and children did the same; then madness came and one man killed another because his cheeks were dry; women struck out and enemy sought enemy and killed, one accusing the other of not showing grief at the king's deprivation. Blood began spattering the ground and staining the huts. Hour after hour people burst with groaning sobs, and Tshaka howled and was like one insane. Death agonies surrendered to the rigid stiffening of limbs and the vultures came in droves and wheeled over the corpses littering the ground; cows moaned because they were swollen with milk and were not relieved; and by midday there was a parching of throats and tears would no longer flow so easily; by late afternoon there was great exhaustion and some crawled to the river to drink and were killed because they thought of their own comfort and did not mourn for the passing of the mother of Tshaka Zulu; and others were executed because they had no more tears and thrust snuff into their eyes; and many greeted death because their tears had dried up and they wiped spit below their eyelids; and by nightfall voices were hoarse from wailing and some were expiring from sheer exhaustion; in the isigodlo women were being choked by the brass rings around their necks and some of them were unable to move owing to the results of their lamentations.

Tshaka, heedless of all this, was able to assuage his thirst and still his hunger but no one else dared. All through the night lamentations poured out and the great song of the AmaZulu was chanted; down by the river where many, forced by thirst, had staggered, even the messengers of death must have become weary for the corpses lay thick; and in the morning light a fearful sight was to be seen: arms and legs had set in horrible, unyielding attitudes; dogs, hyenas and other animals had been at their scavenging and it was as if an enormous number of cannibals had swooped down and not waited to set up cooking-pots. Now there went through the land avengers to destroy those who had not shown sufficient grief; and in far-away kraals people died, and near at hand; and the exhaustion was so great that, had Tshaka's enemies attacked, his might would have been brought low.

Fynn, who had witnessed the carnage, estimated that seven thousand lost their lives. Once he was threatened because he was not weeping but, with his superb courage, he did not quail. Those who had menaced him passed by.

In the light of the westering sun the ground, the land of the AmaZulu, was no less red than the crimson sky; the sudden onrush of darkness brought intense relief by blotting out the scarlet evidence which is left when life is extinguished by violence.

Suddenly, with extraordinary swiftness, Tshaka regained his control; his eyes took in the awful scenes and an impassivity descended upon his features.

'Who has done this?' he demanded.

'The people in their grief,' a counsellor said obsequiously.

'Cowards in their fear,' Tshaka muttered. 'Those out of vengeance,' and the lines from ear to jaw set inflexibly. 'I withdraw my sheltering hands for a little while and you murder amongst yourselves. You behave like irresponsible children. You take life senselessly,' but he did not permit the people to hear his words for much of the carnage had resulted from encouragement given by his counsellors; and the people looked to these men for guidance and respected them. He looked around and said loudly, 'Direct my people to eat and sleep and rest. Let there be no more death except at my command.'

A curious blankness now descended upon the king; not from exhaustion; more as if his deep sorrow had dulled his mental powers. He retired to his hut but the people kept up their wailing and lamentation; and these cries were augmented as more people arrived from every quarter of the land; and every man competed with his neighbour in the turbulence of his expressions of grief.

Amidst great ceremony Nandi was buried, sitting upright, in a hollow made in the wall of an L-shaped grave; the common people might be thrown into the valley of death nearby for the vultures to pick their flesh, but Nandi was the mother of heaven. She was bound into the sitting position and carried out on a mat; the men followed behind her and then came the women, their hands crossed, and there was not a sound save the soft footfalls and now and again a quivering sigh. With Nandi were buried alive young and lovely girls from her retinue, but they were half dead from weariness and suffered less because of that.

One of Tshaka's great counsellors, anxious perhaps to prove his loyalty, arose and asked that for a year no seed should be planted: a year without sowing or reaping, so that the earth should sorrow in desolation and barrenness; the benison of milk should not flow into the mouths of the people, but every drop of milk should be allowed to soak into the soil and feed the hunger of the earth which held within it the body of the mother of heaven; and that all should live in chastity in memory of Nandi; and no man should seek consolation with his wife, and no woman find happiness in the birth of a child, on pain of death.

That evening the cool winds of night blew over a kraal where all, beneath the sway of exhaustion, slept as if dead.

Elsewhere the killing continued until Tshaka's messengers brought word to all in his kindgom.

Yet life did not return to normality: again and again death came so that the land of the AmaZulu might mourn with the son of heaven who was bereft of his mother; and cows who had recently calved were slaughtered so that their calves might discover despair at the loss of their mothers; and recalcitrant tribes who had not come quickly enough to comfort Tshaka and mourn for Nandi met mass death. But now death was controlled and no longer the ill-judged results of foolish, craven efforts; those who died at Tshaka's instigation were more often than not elements of weakness threatening the unity and strength of the nation.

Fynn, who had witnessed the carnage and was now forced to witness further outrages, although on a smaller scale, went around close-mouthed, his features set in horror; and Thola, watching him, saw into his heart and sided with him against Tshaka; and yet she was awed that Tshaka could have loved his mother to such an extraordinary degree. Nandi who, as rumour had it, had been possessed of a tongue sharp enough to cut rhinoceros hide, and a temper to compete with fire blazing through dry grass.

And then, with a sudden revulsion of feeling, Thola felt herself entirely in sympathy with Tshaka again, and completely contemptuous of the white man. What had Fynn to be so self-righteous about?

Sombrely Thola walked down to the river and sat on the bank and stared down into the muddy water.

Was this black king she loved any more cruel than the people in Fynn's bright land of civilisation?

Where in Tshaka's country did spectators pay to view the sufferings of madmen chained to bars; madmen whose crazed minds were further distorted by floggings and maltreatment?

If a woman murdered her husband did the king order that she should have faggots piled around her and did he command that she should meet her death in the agony caused by flames licking her quivering body?

Did he have his people half suffocated by hanging, cut down, and while still alive, drawn and quartered?

Had any man in his kingdom ever slowly strangled to death at the end of a rope – hanged for stealing a crust of bread, a bright bauble – facing and entering eternity because hunger forced hands to snatch at money or food belonging elsewhere?

Those who were executed in civilised lands provided at their hour of death a spectacle for the public; and some were whipped through the streets of towns; and others were flogged at special places under the curious gaze of waiting crowds.

The oceans surrounding Tshaka's country had no ships of the AmaZulu to cast black shadows upon the water, within the holds of those ships men, women and children shackled in slavery; the AmaZulu did not engage in such trafficking, their merchandise was not human beings.

Women and children did not labour in coal mines.

And she thought, wryly, there are no fires made here beneath little chimney sweeps to send them scurrying up dark chimneys.

Death came often, but it came swiftly; and those who survived lived to be a good age. Undernourishment and poverty did not carry them off in their youth; and the dirt and disease of slums were unknown.

Was Fynn up against bestial cruelty or was he up against an alien culture?

If cruelty, then what he condemned as cruelty, was that of a child, merciless indeed; the people were like children. Even she, a primitive in comparison to Fynn, realised that. Tshaka, of course, was not a child, but in him she yet had to discover that exquisite refinement of cruelty which could only stem from an adult mind.

But she knew these thoughts were of the moment; tomorrow, like Fynn, she would probably be criticising the king again.

12

FOR a year a regiment composed of thousands of warriors guarded Nandi's grave; then Tshaka called together the nation and marched towards the sea to that royal kraal called Dukuza. Fynn came up from the settlement at the bay and joined Tshaka who kept the white man at his side; and for the first time in twelve long months real gaiety enlivened the black king's features.

The people of Dukuza came out with singing and acclamation to greet the king but, with Fynn, he turned aside and rested beneath a great fever tree and there put on his war regalia.

A few hours before he had put the courage of the white man to a severe test and he was pleased with Fynn. He had commanded Fynn to swim across a pool in which were crocodile and the white man, not knowing that Tshaka had dozens of warriors poised for action should Fynn be attacked, had stripped himself and braved the reptiles.

'You are a very brave man, my black-tailed finch,' Tshaka observed. 'Do you know that we are about to hold a ceremony of sorrow in honour of the mother who died?'

'No, indeed,' Fynn said, and his face darkened. 'I wish that you would grant me a very great favour.'

'A favour?' The king's eyes swept over the white man. 'What favour?'

'Let no one die. So many have died already.'

'Your courage demands a reward. No one shall die.

Sofili.' He called a counsellor and gave the command. 'This rite of purification will cleanse me and the period of mourning will be over. Remain on the hill, my friend, and your inquisitive eyes will observe all.'

Accompanied by his chiefs Tshaka strode on to Dukuza. The king's steps faltered and he wept in memory of Nandi, his mother, and others wept with him, contorting their faces and crying out loudly; and regiment upon regiment strode up the slopes of the hills surrounding Dukuza so that Tshaka was within the circumference of a great circle made by the bodies of his people; plumes waved in the wind and thousands of voices joined in with the king's lamentation and these cries were augmented by the bellowing of thousands of oxen. When the sun sank behind the hills orders were given that all should rest and cattle were slaughtered and fires made and food cooked; and that day no man lost his life.

When the light of day again spilled in golden effulgence on the tree-dotted hills the rites of purification took place. Gall bladders were torn out of living calves and the regiments and the people massed around Tshaka; and one by one the warriors and the people came up to their king and broke the bladder of gall and sprinkled the contents over him; and this ceremony ate up many hours and the heat of the noonday sun found Tshaka still impassive in his isolated splendour, drenched in bitter, black gall.

Then one of the counsellors spoke to the people.

'The mother of heaven,' he called, 'abides in the land of the spirits and always her vigilance protects the Black One of the AmaZulu, and her thoughts are for the people of her son.

'But, people of the Black One, many there are who have made no lamentation for the mother of heaven; in distant lands men and women laugh and give no

thought to the sorrow in our hearts. The warriors who
have stood watch over the earth-home of the mother of
heaven shall go forth in their thousands and fall upon
these merry-makers and deprive them of their cattle and
the cattle shall symbolise the tears of strange peoples;
and the world will have mourned for the death of the
Great Mother.'

Now the war dance took place and the hills rever-
berated with the echoes of stamping feet and dust
clouds wreathed the trees and trembled above the long
yellowing grasses; the men lifted their voices in song,
but no gentleness was to be found in these songs, and
the glitter of war-fever brought a red glow to the
warriors' eyes, and plumed head-dresses dipped and
swayed.

Now Tshaka made of Dukuza his royal home; and he
sent for the white men and made one of them a captain
of a regiment and ordered that this white man should
take gifts to UmGeorge, the king of the white men, and
procure the precious Macassar oil; and Tshaka sent
men and women of his people with the white man,
King, so that UmGeorge might see for himself how
splendid were the people of the AmaZulu. Among those
who accompanied King was Hlambamanzi, known to
the white men as Jacob.

Thola was greatly tempted to disillusion Tshaka about
the qualities of Macassar oil, but Fynn had already
expressed his doubts regarding the potency of the oil
and had only succeeded in making Tshaka even more
determined to procure this medicine. What with the
year of mourning and Tshaka's many activities she had
gradually become reconciled to her ineffectuality and
could not find the courage anyway to brave a recurrence
of Tshaka's displeasure. She was also aware of an under-
current of tension in the kraal and heard vague murmurs about a smelling-out of witches; and she trembled

when her thoughts returned to the desecration she had perpetrated on the king's person at the time of the birth of UmuSa's child. An action which had then appeared simple and innocent now assumed hideous proportions. Who would believe that she had intended Tshaka no harm; who would remember UmuSa as a gentle, simple woman, agonising in childbirth, pleading for strengthening medicine for a child who had no hope of life?

She was aware that she was being watched narrowly by many and that the old midwives who had attended UmuSa always averted their heads in her presence and passed her in a scurrying panic; and in the dark hours of night sly whispers suggested that evil-doers were loose in the land of the AmaZulu; the sister of Umbopha sent long-lidded, covert glances at Thola, and the more timid of the women avoided this girl whom the Black One had given the name of Flower of Maturity.

Then fear was swallowed up by excitement and, on Thola's part, fear for Tshaka's safety; rumours circulated that the king was about to march on the Ama-Pondo, the people whose country lay beyond the settlement beside the bay where the white men lived. Young men came to request spears of Tshaka and they received their weapons amidst much ceremony and, later, feasting and dancing.

Tshaka, more splendid than ever, danced with his warriors and sang a song he had lately composed in which subtle allusions to his unhappy childhood boded ill for anyone unwise enough to gainsay him now that he was at the height of his power; and his warriors responded, calling him the swiftest of blades; a shining blade, swifter than the winds, whose edge glittered with the sharpness and power of silver lightning; a blade, which when used against the foe, vibrated with the massive rumbling of thunder; a blade which drank up blood as the sea absorbs the river, as the dry earth receives the cooling drops of rain. And they saluted Tshaka with the royal salute and in their strong voices swore that only death would stop them in their defence of him and that, should he fall, they would die upon his body. And every man spoke truth.

Then the female regiments danced, a strange, shuffling dance, and their high, clear, soprano voices cut shrilly through the heat-laden air; the men's eyes glittered and some of them looked discreetly at the ground and Tshaka smiled his gentle smile. Each woman held a little spear, a miniature of the warriors' weapon of war, and wielded the small assegai with grace and precision; presently Tshaka leapt into the midst of the women and danced magnificently with them; and his people were entranced by the splendid proportions of his body and the litheness of his movements; and even the women faltered, as if they knew that his presence brought insipidity to their posturings.

The sun travelled forward across the rolling hills and when the sea lay shrouded in evening mists light still dappled the western sky in orange-gold streamers. Summons came for Thola to attend the king at his evening meal and as she followed the guard to the royal hut she was suddenly poignantly aware, more so perhaps than ever before, of the vastness and untracked strangeness of Africa; it was as if the land was clothed in unreality; as if such silence, such awful, alien remoteness could not exist. Even the sea-wind, laden with a clammy saltiness, held within its whispering sounds a mysterious potency; as if it had blown across great, water-swept distances and absorbed unearthly properties; and when the moon rose like a flame in the black sky shadows became dread things; and every sigh and whisper premonitory murmurings of doom.

She shivered and was suddenly terribly afraid, irrationally so, but reason provided no armour. Intuitively she felt that Dukuza was a place of sorrow and tragedy, yet its history was cleaner. Far more blood had flowed at Tshaka's other kraals; Bulawayo had seen the slaughter of thousands in one day. Her imagination thronged the darkness with threatening shadows and when she approached the royal hut she saw that swirling mist was eddying around the contours of the walls; some distance away the great euphorbia tree under which Tshaka often sat loomed out of the mist-wreaths and the moon-shadows beneath it possessed a dimensional blackness; when the wind parted the branches and moved them the traceries of silver drawn by the light of the moon caused the blackness to writhe and contort and she was reminded of the huge snakes which coiled themselves around their prey and constricted and crushed.

She crawled into Tshaka's presence but even here she sensed a tension and the brave flicker of firelight could not dissipate her foreboding; and the flames seemed to paint the king in red blood; and the shadows cast by the flaring light were grotesquely elongated so that even her own shadow seemed to menace the king. The warm, smoke-filled air flowed around her but did not comfort her and the smoke-wraiths made her remember the tendril-like, wispy mist in the dark outside. She bent before Tshaka and a long shiver shook her again.

'You are cold, my flower,' he observed, but there was a vagueness in his voice and when he drew her to him she felt that he was not truly aware of his own actions.

'I do not like this place, Lord,' she murmured. 'I do not like Dukuza. Must we live here? There are so many other...'

Such women's nonsense he ignored.

'Perhaps,' he teased, 'you would like me to marry you off to some inland chief? Then you will be far away from Tshaka and the sea.'

She let her head rest against his massive shoulder and her limbs relaxed; and his nearness obliterated her fears.

'I have remembered,' the king remarked, and she was lulled by his deep, easy breathing, 'that you once had a dream about an infection beneath the nails of my hand.'

Despite herself her muscles knotted and she knew that the king was aware of her rigidity; his hands came to her throat, caressingly, as if he wished to soothe her.

'I did nothing about that dream, my flower, for any action would have involved you. In the past I have told you that I place my trust in you.'

Silence quickly followed upon his words and it seemed as if he were waiting for her to speak. She could not.

'That was the time when one of my sisters gave birth to a child,' Tshaka continued at last. 'There is a story that medicine made from the scrapings of my body was given to the child. Has this rumour reached your ears, my flower?'

The rasping of her throat seemed to echo through the stillness.

'I see that this has not happened. Speak truth to me now, my flower; do not betray my trust. There is no one to hear your words.'

And she realised suddenly that for the very first time she was entirely alone with the king.

'Rumour has it,' Tshaka said, his voice devoid of expression, 'that you obtained the scrapings from me.'

Again the stillness descended and it seemed as if the king was intensely alert to her reaction; his hands lay quiet upon her and a pause came in his breathing.

'Surely you do not believe . . . you do not believe that harm could come to you through . . . through scrapings . . .' she whispered, forcing a light, mocking, carelessness into her tones.

Now the king moved impatiently.

'For all the brilliance of your mind you are sometimes a fool,' he said, almost roughly. 'Often I have explained to you it is not what I believe but what my people believe. Can I permit a rumour that a woman tricked me? Bewitched me? If I permit that others will try, and death comes along many paths other than witchcraft. I wish you to answer me, Thola. We are alone.'

'Are we alone, Lord, because you think I will admit such a thing? Would you not have me killed?'

He sighed deeply.

'You have instilled a weakness in me, Thola. You, of all, I wish to have loyal.' His fingers gripped her head and his strength seemed about to crush her temples. 'Answer me,' he ordered brusquely. 'Answer me!'

She could not bear to destroy his trust.

'I did not betray you, Lord,' she said, investing each word with slow sincerity; and only then did she understand how much his suspicions had troubled him for he grasped her convulsively and the sweet delight of his nearness carried with it a bruising pain.

'Ah, Thola,' he murmured against her throat, 'small one, never betray me,' and in the great tide of her love for him she had no thought of tomorrow and felt herself so entirely his possession that nothing in her was left to yield to him; and again there came a pause in his deep breathing, and a stillness, as if he gathered together all his resources; and a surging strength overcame the unsteadiness of his hands; gradually, slowly, as if separation brought to him an ache, a pain-filled longing, he pushed her away from him. So dazed, so drugged that the world was whirling chaos, she murmured plaintively and sought to return to him, but the sure strength of his hands held her away, and when she opened her eyes he was smiling down at her.

'Small one,' he said, 'my love for you proves itself,' and the tenderness of his voice was like an intimate caress. 'Even against myself I keep you secure.'

'If I were ruler of this country,' Thola said, 'the country and the people would not matter against you ... would not matter ...'

'And yet to the one who gave the medicine to UmuSa, UmuSa's happiness was of greater importance,' Tshaka observed wryly.

His face swam above her, the oriental eyes too penetrating, terrifying. Was he amusing himself? Did he know she had lied? Did he *know*? And would knowledge of her betrayal permit his love to survive?

'I have not harmed you, Lord,' she cried desperately. 'I would not harm you!'

Immediately his face softened, and he bent over her again; half fainting she closed her eyes and thought she heard him groan, thought she felt the touch of his hands upon her cheeks, and the next moment was immeasurably humiliated as his even tones calmly summoned the servants; even more so when food was brought in and the king ate with a hearty appetite.

'You have too much self-control,' she flung at him angrily, wanting to spit and stamp her feet in fury. 'You are made of iron ... of stone ... of ... of ...'

'Warm, human flesh,' he said and laughed, and the laughter creases around his eyes deepened. 'You had better sit up, my flower. You have never learnt to eat while lying down. I do not want you to choke.'

'I would choke on food anyway,' she spat.

'All the same you will eat,' Tshaka said and muttered an order and a servant held out a great gob of meat.

Stubbornly she defied him.

'Eat,' he said again, his voice very soft and gentle, and the red devils came to dwell in his eyes.

For one long moment she pitted her will against his;

then she took the meat and bit into it, and his soft laughter brought her bitterness.

'I am choking,' she cried, 'I *am*.'

'Choke then,' Tshaka said and leisurely accepted more grilled meat. 'Choke then, my smallest one,' and he smiled at her; against her inclination she was conquered and she smiled back, companionably; and now warmth filled the hut and the wild darkness outside was tamed by this man whose strength was unbounded, whose mind shone with the light of genius, whose might subjugated whatever tried to stand against him, whose love anchored her in a haven of deepest peace.

And love became again a yearning tenderness, a desire to protect and bless, to give, to soothe, to keep for always in sure security.

13

In the still hours of the night Tshaka Zulu rose up and departed with his warriors to make war on the Ama-Pondo; after a day's march he came to one of his smaller kraals and there he sat himself down under a great euphorbia tree and reviewed his troops. Later generations called this place Shaka's Kraal. Some distance away was a rock which they called Chaka's Rock and around this rock they built a legend and said that here the Black One's warriors jumped down into the boulder-gashed sea at his command. They said that the king thus ordered death for his enjoyment and delight; but this was not so. The cowards he plucked from his army and destroyed, and his warriors understood this action and revered it, for they knew that he was totally without cowardice: always in battle he called 'Follow me!', never did they have to wait for him. But his tried warriors, those brave men who either won victory or died in the attempt, these he guarded zealously; he rewarded them with many heads of cattle; he was to· wards their families as a father; and this they knew: he never asked of them what he could not do himself.

After the regiments had rested and eaten the march was continued; Tshaka rose up and the soles of his feet ate up the miles and presently the white man, Fynn, came up to meet the king, for Fynn had been advised of Tshaka's arrival.

Darkness was again falling and Tshaka had settled down for the night; around him were counsellors and personal servants and a contingent of warriors, but the bulk of his army were encamped some distance in the rear.

The king made Fynn welcome and talked to him far into the night until the sleepy Fynn was hard pressed to restrain his yawns; and then Tshaka sent the white man to his bed, and his low, rumbling laugh followed Fynn into the darkness.

In the morning the impi proceeded on and came to one of Fynn's residences where Fynn handed over supplies of corn at Tshaka's good-humoured suggestion; a day later the army swarmed over the banks of the Umzimkulu and made itself comfortable; here stood a house which Fynn had built, and an enclosure for cattle; Fynn eyed the hordes with some despair, accepted the inevitable and sought Tshaka out.

'I have told the herd-boys to drive the cattle past here,' Fynn said. 'I hope you will choose a beast' – and at Tshaka's derisive smile, the white man chuckled reluctantly – 'beasts, I suppose.'

'It is customary for a host to act with generosity,' Tshaka said and laughed. 'My friend, dispense with that look of desolation. I will not rob you,' and he chose seventeen cattle.

Now he called his impi to attention and the warriors took their places. The doctors came and strengthened the men for war; then Tshaka strode into the midst of the impi and addressed them.

'Many tears have fallen from these eyes,' he said in his deep voice. 'Many sighs have escaped these lips. Tears and sighs for the mother who is no more.'

In their bass rumble the warriors echoed his words.

'You have been told of the peoples who did not weep with me, who did not mourn my great loss. Now the time has come for the great elephant to trample them beneath his feet so that they may learn of pain and share sorrow. Hear my command, my warriors! Eat up all

155

those before me; let all those between me and the land of the white men kiss the earth. Build a pathway for me to the land of the white men. You know that I have sent wise men to their land to prepare the white men for my approach – my friendly approach – therefore make this pathway even and easily traversed for me!'

The army roared its approval and that war-madness fell upon them; that red-eyed, evil-mask look came to them; they brandished their assegais and rattled their shields and stamped their feet and thundered out the royal salute: 'Bayete! Bayete! Bayete, InKosi!'

And Tshaka privately issued orders that white men were not to be attacked. The regiments moved off and as the days passed messengers returned to Tshaka and reported military movements and Tshaka received the tidings of each victory with calm acceptance.

'Nevertheless,' he observed to Fynn, who was still unhappily acting as host, 'the commander of the army is a fool.'

'Then you should relieve him of his command,' Fynn remarked. 'Your warriors will lose their confidence in him.'

'He acts on my instructions,' Tshaka said. 'My orders curtail his foolishness. He is my mouth, therefore he will be respected. Ah, my friend, I fear I must place the majority of my people in that category. Foolish children. Are you not foolish children?' and he smiled at his attendant counsellors.

'We are fools indeed,' they hastened to agree, and added, 'And Sofili too.'

'They say you are a fool as well,' Tshaka told Fynn. 'You are, my black-tailed finch,' much to the white man's chagrin.

But the moment he was alone with Fynn he unbent.

'You are a brave man, my friend, and a wise one. I do not wish my people to hear me admit that. Let them respect you a little and fear you not at all for the people with white skins are a great danger to them. A grave and great danger,' he added sombrely.

'I am compelled to point out,' Fynn said, with much spirit and not a little pomposity, 'that your strategy might be termed foolish too. You are warring with the tribes bordering on the white men's land. That will not convince the white men of your peaceful intentions, believe me.'

'I do believe you,' the king said quietly. 'I do not look for help to the people of your race. They await their opportunity.' He stared before him unseeingly. 'Certainly I could not afford their attacking me. The time is not ripe; my foolish children, my people who are as children, have much to learn. Fynn,' and the penetrating eyes swept over the white man, 'you know this chief against whom I have sent my warriors. If I suggested peace would Faku be willing to become a vassal?'

'I should think so. As an inducement you might return the women your warriors captured; you might order that food should not be destroyed.'

'That shall be done,' and he gave immediate orders; and Faku came under Tshaka's control and the king sent his new vassal gifts of cattle and these cattle came from the herds which Tshaka's warriors had captured from the people of Faku.

Fynn, despite his innate kindheartedness and his sympathy for Faku, could not repress a burst of laughter; and when news came of the returning army's approach he was permitted further insight into the character of the unpredictable Tshaka Zulu.

He heard Tshaka abusing the messengers; he heard him demanding the reason why the impi had not cleared a path right up to the white men's country; the army had failed and was in disgrace. The warriors feared to approach Tshaka; miserably they camped some distance away, surrounded by thousands of cattle which they had taken from the enemy; and they starved rather than touch their plunder.

Tshaka left them to suffer for two days; then he instructed a counsellor to drive cattle to them to be slaughtered for food.

'But,' he said, his face stern, although the laughter wrinkles around his eyes were creasing deeply, 'let them not know that the cattle come from me. Berate them for their disgrace. Instruct them to kill the cattle and fill their stomachs but command them to say that these cattle died from their weariness. Let them believe that the cattle come from you. Fynn, you may accompany my Induna, but on peril of your life do not reveal my soft-heartedness.'

After the army had eaten he permitted them into his presence where they were cleansed of the blood of war and sent down to the waters of the sea so that they might bathe their bodies and wash away all contamination; and when they returned Tshaka sang a song he had composed and sadness came to him and he remembered his mother; and the army mourned with him.

Tshaka now started on his return journey, to Fynn's well-concealed relief, and when he arrived at the banks of the Umzimkulu he was concerned for the little boys, the mat carriers, fearing that they might drown. He went into the surging waters and made of himself a bulwark; his chiefs and warriors followed his example. For ninety minutes he remained in the turbulent water, helping the boys and the calves across, and afterwards he had fires made so that warmth could be instilled into the bedraggled little objects.

Yet that night Fynn, who was accompanying Tshaka on his journey, heard him give an order for a woman who had committed a petty theft to be executed; and the following day a laggard warrior provided an example for the impi and was stabbed; and when Tshaka gave the command for the man to die he turned his head away and Fynn saw that the king did not wish others to witness the troubled sorrow this deed brought to him. Nor did Tshaka spare himself: as the journey unfolded several more warriors died.

Then Tshaka came upon little herd-boys who had the care of cattle; he looked beyond the droves of cattle and let his gaze rest upon Dukuza which was visible in the distance; and he called the little boys closer and they came tremblingly although they pretended manly courage. They squatted at his feet and kept their anxious eyes lowered.

'No doubt,' Tshaka said gently, 'you are most careful of the cattle.'

Stammeringly they assured him that they were.

'You are especially careful of the cows who have recently calved.'

A flat silence followed this statement.

'As it happens, you are little ones yourselves yet you cause the baby calves suffering for you steal their milk from their mothers. Is that not so?'

Again their only reply was silence.

'I do not think you will grow up to be the kind of warriors this land requires. You know your task: it is to preserve the riches of the land, the cattle. If, as children, you cannot be trusted in simple tasks, how can you be trusted to protect and keep secure the nation?'

The king bent his gaze upon them and a deep furrow pulled his brows together and he sighed once; and then, as if by force of will, he smiled and said with great gentleness, 'Such as you will only help to destroy what has been built up. Swear to me on the great oath that you have not deprived the small calves of milk.'

But they were guilty and had not the courage to

swear so great an oath.

Now beads of sweat appeared on the king's forehead and even Fynn turned away from the suffering naked on the king's face.

'Go to my warriors,' Tshaka continued, smiling again, 'and tell them that you are not fit to live and must die, but tell them also that the king is of this mind: you are as brave as if you were grown men, and you are honourable and do not lie.'

The little boys saluted the king and, after a farewell glance at the cattle, walked to meet the army, and they died.

Fynn opened his mouth but, as the king's tortured eyes fell upon him, he closed his lips and dropped his head.

At evenfall they entered Dukuza. The king was received with great joy and the Zulu chant of war rolled over the encircling hills and faded away and was engulfed by the night-silence of Africa. Fynn spent the early part of the evening with Tshaka and then, wearied out, sought sleep; the following day he returned to his settlement at the bay.

Tshaka, extraordinarily restless, sent his impi off to war again, this time against Soshangena whose stronghold lay hundreds of miles away. So few warriors remained at Dukuza that he had the youths, the mat carriers, brought back and of these striplings he brought into being a new regiment: the Regiment of the Bees.

'Who shall sting for me,' the king said and laughed. 'Their honey shall be for my delectation and their stings shall bring death to my enemies.'

A sadness lay heavily upon him and this gloom overshadowed the whole of Dukuza; people spoke in whispers and slunk about the huts in the way of sly beasts. Tshaka composed a song in which he complained of the afflictions placed upon him and his

160

people shuddered when it seemed that he was so sorely troubled that he welcomed the thought of death.

In the isigodlo Umbopha's sister openly declared that the Black One was bewitched; and she watched Thola and smiled secretly to herself.

Then the king had a dream: the ship which had taken his people to UmGeorge no longer rode the water triumphantly, but moved slowly; and in the dream the king saw that the masts were shattered. Despite himself he was distressed.

Soon afterwards the ship did indeed return to the settlement at the bay; King, who had been in command of the expedition, was grievously ill and the other white men came up to Dukuza without him; and with them came the men and women who had been sent by Tshaka to UmGeorge.

It transpired that Tshaka's emissaries had only met UmGeorge's representative, not in England, but in Algoa Bay, and were little impressed with what they had seen and with the manner in which they had been handled.

'The kingdom of UmGeorge is as nothing,' the chiefs told Tshaka respectfully. 'All that we saw there we have seen here. We were asked many questions; we were required to know the Great Elephant's plans and when the Black One plans to attack,' and they trembled. 'We gave no reply; can dogs know the Black One's mind? We decided then to return to our father as quickly as possible to let him know the anxiety in the thoughts of the white men concerning his movements; one of us tried to escape to return the more speedily, but this was not accomplished. The white man who acted as our guardian in the strange land was as a father to us, yet we did not believe he could hold the shield of protection over us.'

'Be that as it may,' Tshaka thundered, 'you have,

without a doubt, returned with the Macassar oil?'

'No, lord,' the chiefs whimpered, 'no, lord, for the people of UmGeorge had none.'

Then the king's wrath was terrible to witness, for he smiled and he spoke with gentleness; when that was the case with Tshaka many deaths could be expected; and the pallor of the white men increased and they moved restlessly.

'So it is,' the Black One said: and he turned to white faces and frowned. 'My ivory has been taken but in return I receive – a present,' and his voice cut with venom. 'A present I did not request and do not want. I am not interested in gewgaws. I do not need to deck myself out to convince others that I am king. You protest your friendship for me, but what I ask you refuse. Excuse after excuse is made. You are dogs; worse than dogs: you are jackals, turned white with cowardice, scum, scavengers. May I sleep with my sister if I do not repent of the friendship I have shown you.'

The white men begged leave to explain and tried to convince the king that the oil had not been available; as soon as it was procurable supplies would be sent to Tshaka immediately.

'You,' said Tshaka, pointing to a white man, John Cane, 'shall immediately go to those in authority. They must be told how I have been humiliated by your persisting in denying me what I ask. No one does that to Tshaka. No, indeed. You will go and convey to those above you that my heart is black with anger. My hands are hard upon my assegai; my patience is no more. Get from my sight, you worthless ones!'

He remained incensed but when one of the white men died he expressed sympathy; at least the man had died a natural death and had not been helped home by the people of heaven. As death was a defilement the white men came and cleansed Tshaka with gall, and then they were permitted to leave.

And then Tshaka dreamed: in his dream, while he was dallying with one of his sisters, a dog climbed upon the roof of the hut and barked.

'Which is a bad omen,' he remarked to Thola; then, reprovingly, 'I see you are not yet wearing the brass collars I gave you. You are a perverse, stubborn and ungrateful woman.'

'But, Lord, I love you beyond words.'

'So you say. You have done nothing to prove your love. Others testify their loyalty and love as they die – by my command – but you . . . you come into my presence and speak as if you possess the wisdom of the world; and you tremble when I touch you. That is all.'

'Send me not to death so that I may protest my love as I die. You know I would do that. I would much rather live, Lord, and please you.'

'Is it pride that makes you believe you please me?' He embraced her and she did, indeed, tremble. 'See. Talk and tremble, that is all,' and he laughed gently. 'But you do please me. My flower, I have had this bad dream. The whisper of witchcraft continues to go from mouth to mouth among my people. Now you shiver. Are you then cold? I think it is expedient to call together the soothsayers and the diviners and find out what the meaning of my dream may be. Perhaps there are some around who speak of love but dream of hate and death. Is that so, do you think?'

'Lord, do you believe in soothsayers and diviners? Sometimes innocent people are accused.' Thola shivered and turned her head away. 'And sometimes innocent people die.'

'Mostly,' Tshaka said, 'innocent people die. As a result others who might conspire against me think twice. They become exceedingly careful and obedient. It is a bad thing for a dog to climb upon the roof of a hut and bark. That is a sure sign of witchcraft. You do not believe? Perhaps you are the one who is practising witchcraft. You have extraordinary courage. That I know.'

'I would not harm you, Lord. You are my life.'

'Often the one who is being used is unaware that he – or she – is the instrument.' Thoughtfully he fingered his chin. 'I will call together my people from every corner of the land and we shall see who is doing bad deeds. And I will call all the diviners, both male and female. The diviners will act with infinite care for I once taught them a hard lesson.'

'Tell me of it, Lord,' Thola said, and the fear inspired by the thought of a smelling-out ceremony roughened her voice.

'I smeared blood upon the posts of my hut late at night when there were no eyes to see my actions. Then I called out that I had been bewitched, and no one doubted for I had acted in great secrecy. My nation was assembled and the diviners ran amongst the people and found many guilty. All day they sought out the guilty ones and hit at these with tails of hair. When the farce began to weary me I stood up before those assembled and I said that I had put the blood upon the posts. I had wished to discover how real is the power of the diviners.

'As it happened, some diviners had not found a single person guilty but had kept their eyes on me. I commanded them to move away from the other soothsayers. I looked at those who had been found guilty and I said to my people, "Fall now upon the soothsayers, the false readers of life, and slay them," and the deceivers died.'

'Then, Lord, if you do not believe, why call together the people? If you do, many will die. Why send them to their death?'

'You remain obtuse, my flower,' and he laughed into her throat where the skin was supple and whole and not disfigured by brass rings. 'After the diviners have been busy most people will be afraid even to think. Will you be afraid, my dearest love?'

'I know nothing of witchcraft. If I were the most powerful witch in the world I still would not harm you. I do not think you need fear witchcraft. I fear your brothers.'

'Brothers?' Tshaka repeated. 'I have only one brother, the son of my mother, Ngwadi.'

'I know that the sons of your father are not known as your brothers. But although no one dares call them your brothers, you still cannot escape the fact that they are. I do not trust Dingane and Mhlangana. They are always inseparable and they are too friendly with Umbopha. I do not trust him either. They are servile in your presence but I think they scheme together. They would like to rule the land of the AmaZulu.'

'Both of them?' Tshaka said and smiled gently. 'Do not be misled. They fear me and they fear each other. Should I be left behind . . .'

'You always use that phrase. Only men killed in battle are said to be left behind.'

'If I must die that is how I would wish to lose life. Should I die, do you imagine they would remain inseparable? Each would wield a knife and seek the other's ribs.'

'Do you trust them?'

'No, my flower. But I do not fear them. Mhlangana is a fool and Dingane is besotted with women. When he is able to tear himself away from the pleasures of love his whole mind is bent upon his belly. Already he is as fat as a pregnant woman. Ngwadi would never harm me. He has proved his loyalty many times. He cleared the pathway to the Zulu people for me by removing the son of my father. He will fight to the death for me.'

'That is so, Lord,' Thola agreed, and sighed; the king appeared to forget her presence and sat in deep contemplation; presently the furrows bit deeply into the smoothness between his brows and he sighed.

'You are grieved, Lord.'

'I will not call the diviners,' Tshaka said heavily. 'Not yet. I will act as diviner myself and remove those who speak so glibly of witchcraft. Most whispers originate where women are gathered together. I have seen the sly glances,' and his penetrating gaze fastened on Thola. 'To that an end will be put. Harden yourself, my flower, for you will soon witness much shedding of blood.'

14

THE king summoned women to him, from the isigodlo
and from the surrounding countryside; the sisters from
the isigodlo came with happiness in their hearts, never
suspecting the trial that awaited them; and the women
of the people came wonderingly and without fear.

The counsellors sat around the king, ready to applaud
his every action, their servile countenances reflecting
his changing moods; when he smiled gently at the
waiting women, they smiled as well; and when he
frowned their faces grew dark and lowering.

Thola, who had not been called for questioning but
who was in attendance, crouched close by; the warm
summer sun streamed down on her but did not relax
her limbs and when the king's features became benign
apprehension brought a rising nausea to her.

'Whispers have come to my ears,' Tshaka said; his
lips smiled but there were no laughter creases around
his eyes. 'It seemed to me that I was in the midst of a
forest and that every leaf on the branch of every tree
was rustling. These murmurs had the soft sound of
women's voices. You will agree with me that this is a
mystery.'

'Our Father,' the women said. 'Great Black One!'

'These whispers have disturbed me,' the king continued. 'I do not favour words that are said softly
behind a guarding hand.'

The women dropped their eyes and many sighed;
and on foreheads a fine film of sweat appeared; trickles

of wetness ran down beneath their arms and a restlessness possessed them.

'You,' Tshaka said to one of his sisters, and the girl fell on her knees before him, 'have a certain slyness; your eyes peer this way and that and you scarcely move your lips when you speak. Are you a witch?'

The girl's throat muscles worked convulsively.

'Are you a witch?' the king repeated, his smile almost gay as if he were indulging in a mild joke. 'Come, my sister, let me have your answer. Do not keep secrets from your king. Reveal what is in your mind to him. Are you a witch?'

'No, Lord,' the girl replied, the words coming stiffly from her tongue.

'You shall die,' the king said very softly.

When servants leaped at the girl Thola thought Tshaka would turn coward and command that she be killed elsewhere; just for a moment the smile left his mouth; then he mastered himself and sat impassively as the club smashed down on the girl's skull.

Next he questioned an older woman.

'Are you happy?' he asked.

'I am happy, Lord,' the woman quavered.

She died swiftly.

'Are you filled with happiness?' he demanded of the girl who had stood at this woman's side.

'I am sad, Great One.'

She too died very quickly.

Some he spared and the women tried to give the same answers as these had given; but whatever reply was given it was obvious that the king's whim and not the answer determined whether life should continue.

When the midday sun shone down in fiery heat a pile of corpses lay near the king and the air was fetid with the smell of death; the women wilted in the heat; limbs trembled and exhaustion and fear brought a greyness to their skins; some could not control themselves and wept piteously.

'Return to your homes,' Tshaka ordered, smiling at the women. 'Whisper no more.'

A breeze from the sea swept over Dukuza but could not clear the air of the smell of death and even when the dead were removed the odour lingered and a dog sniffed and licked at the damp, oily places staining the ground. Later in the afternoon black clouds banked along the horizon and the heat became sticky and humid and rivulets of sweat ran down black bodies. Surges of thunder made a tumult in the valleys and above the hill-tops the lightning had a strange ochre glow; soon the darkness was as if it were the hour of twilight and when rain swept down from the shrouded sky the gloom intensified.

The king, while not overwhelmed by primitive terror, was nevertheless not entirely at ease; in the royal hut he lay on his skin rugs, surrounded by twittering isigodlo women. Thola remained a little apart and the king did not call her nearer. At a particularly vicious thunder-clap she winced and was obscurely annoyed when Tshaka noticed her slight shudder; his eyes flicked over her and the gravity of his expression was lightened by the slight creasing of laughter wrinkles fanning out towards his temples. When he put a hand on one of the girls beside him, Thola turned her head away fastidiously and the king's low laughter rumbled through the hut; a few minutes later he said, 'My Flower!'

'Yes, Lord?' Stubbornly she kept her head averted.

'You are not comfortable.'

'This place is full of death and violence,' she said and this time she looked at the king and her stubborn pride would not allow her to cringe; bitterness filled her voice. 'At least I do not whisper,' she added and expected his eyes to blaze; he frowned slightly but he was not angered. 'The heavens will not have to weep for me as they are weeping for those whose silly malicious whispers earned them shattered skulls today.'

Awed gasps escaped the women and the men servants arched forward, ready to drag Thola away; but Tshaka pointed to the shadowed corner of the hut and the women crept into the dimness; then he motioned for the men to leave.

'Come here,' he said to Thola and she obeyed unsteadily. He swept her down beside him and took her face between his hands and his fingers pressed deeply into her flesh, bruising the bones of her cheeks. 'Fool,' he said, his voice very low. 'You fool! Need you be told that those whispers were directed against you?'

'I do not want others to die on my account.'

'A noble statement,' the king said, 'but if these foolish women convince the people that you have indeed bewitched me you will die on your own account – and I as well. I am reconciled to the fact that you obtain some extraordinary satisfaction in your criticisms of me. Be quiet. That I mean. Now listen carefully. Do not permit your courage to run away with you again when others are present. Do you understand, Thola?'

'I understand that tomorrow a hundred more will die.'

'No,' the king said, 'two hundred.'

'Because you are angry with me!'

'You flatter yourself. Two hundred will die because it is expedient that they die. But let this trouble your sleep. It is expedient that they die because you have endangered my safety.'

'You stoop low when you murder women.'

His hands dropped from her face and caught her shoulders and held her strongly.

'Thola,' he said, 'Thola, do not try me too far.'

'You have tried me too far,' she muttered. 'I cannot bear your touch. I know it is only the firelight but you look as if you are smeared with blood. And I know that I am unimportant and that Tshaka does not care how he affects me. I know that the crook of your little finger can bring death to me...'

'Be quiet. I must call you fool again. By my sister, it is a terrible thing when a woman such as you is a weakness in a man.'

'I do not believe any more that you kill for the sake of your people. You kill for your own delight. You are on the way to being a bloodthirsty madman. You are just a savage after all. Besides, you are afraid of lightning.'

'I would be as much a fool as you were I not afraid of lightning.'

'Let me go. I told you I cannot bear your touch. You are right. I must be crazed. I was so crazed I thought I loved you. You are a black savage and I despise you. Let me go or I will shout out at the top of my voice that I despise you and then you will *have* to kill me.'

'No, indeed,' the king said dryly, 'I do not have to kill you. I will kill the boy who brought you to me,' and his hands were suddenly very gentle on her shoulders. Despite the terrible glitter in his eyes she saw that he had his anger under strict control; and, as if by magic, her own anger was swept away. She wanted to grovel at his feet and beg his forgiveness.

'Now you will not believe me when I say I did not mean my words,' she cried despairingly. 'You will think I have changed for Malanga's sake.'

'That I will,' Tshaka said and sighed. 'And you cannot bear to be near to me. You shall decide how near you wish to be to me. One word from you, my flower, and I will release you. Instantly.' He looked towards the other women. 'Go,' he said gently and one by one the women crept out of the hut. He called to a servant and the fire was replenished and a gust of wind swept in and the servant's shadow fell distortedly on the walls of the hut as the tongues of flame leapt up; outside the thunder growled and lightning flashed over the countryside.

'Go, if you wish,' he said to Thola. 'I do not want you to remain because of Malanga. I will not take his life this time. But if you are indiscreet again he will have to die.'

'It is not because of Malanga that I remain here,' Thola said and shivered. She was scarcely conscious of herself; every power of attention was focused on the king and, even at his command, she could not have moved away from him. When his arms encircled her it was as if she had entered her own home and had closed the door against the world.

'Say the word,' Tshaka murmured, his lips against her ear. 'Shall I release you now, little one?'

She sighed his name and did not know that she was weeping.

'And now, my flower? And now?'

'Do not let me go,' she pleaded and heard herself sob.

'Not even now?' The tenderness in his voice was a caress in itself and, like a small animal seeking warmth, she burrowed closer to him; the next moment he pushed her away so precipitately that she sprawled on the floor of the hut; and, momentarily, she was an awkward and ungainly figure. With difficulty she levered herself onto her knees and stared blindly at the king; the wavering outlines of his face swam before her; when, at last, she was able to see clearly she put up a hand as if to shield herself from the king's eyes.

'Understand me, Thola,' the king said coldly, 'you have not conquered me. No one conquers Tshaka.'

Slowly her hand dropped away and she crouched before the king.

'I am aware of my weaknesses. You are one. But a weakness can be changed into a form of strength. You are a woman of very great courage, as I have told you before, and I respect your courage. This I must also say to you. I do not think you will know how great is my love for you.' His voice became even colder. 'And how great is my desire for you.' His hands, when he opened his snuff-container and pinched up a few grains of snuff, were perfectly steady. 'In point of fact,' he added quietly, 'you have complicated life in many, many ways.'

'I am sorry, Lord.'

'You are not in the least sorry. You have a gloating look of happiness at the thought that you have the power to disturb me. That, my flower, is not because you love me. That look comes, I think, from satisfied vanity. Your vanity will cost many of my people their lives.'

'Oh, you know that isn't true,' Thola cried indignantly.

'Never overawed,' Tshaka said, half smiling at her. 'Never overawed. There is not a man in my kingdom who does not crawl at my feet, but you defy me.'

'The men aren't in love with you. I am,' Thola said with spirit.

And Tshaka laughed, his deep laughter ringing through the hut. He stretched out a hand and quite roughly pulled her to him and held her so that she could not move.

'Ah, Thola,' he said and sighed, 'how can I let you go? Tomorrow you had better say you have a pain' – and his eyes travelled over her body and he laughed again – 'and remain on your sleeping-mat. That way you will not be a witness to my bloodthirstiness and I will be spared dour looks and a sullen reception when I call you to me in the evening. Thola,' he ran a finger gently along her chin and pinched her lower lip, 'do not cause more trouble.'

She lay against him, savouring the sweetness of the

moment. 'I do not mean to cause trouble, Lord. Before I know what has happened I say things I regret afterwards.'

'That is so,' the king agreed, his voice full of gentle, teasing laughter. 'You have very little control over yourself. Is that not so, my smallest one? Even now,' and his voice deepened.

'Even now,' she whispered.

'I have a dream. I dream of a day when all is safe and the future secure.' Tshaka eased her onto the skin rugs as if seeking, unconsciously, to rest her body in a warm and comfortable position. 'The realisation of my dream will mean a great deal to me. Be sure that you are with me that moment, Thola. Be sure.'

Outside the storm had spent its violence and the rain now fell softly, purling in misty greyness over the hills; the wind fluted in the trees gradually changed direction then rushed in great puffs, blowing down from the high, cold mountains, and a chill crept into the air. With the first hint of snow autumn colours would flame and then winter would come and gather up the yellow and orange leaves and turn the grass into pallid stretches of dunness. The days and nights would be cold; rain would cease to fall; birds would fly away in search of warmth; and many animals and insects would go into a deep sleep; then, as if seeking to keep summer at bay, the strong winds would come; the winds would howl from early morning until late at night; cease for a little space, gather strength and moaningly usher in another day. The sands along the sea shore would be blown into stinging surges. And then, suddenly, summer would burn the land in fierce heat; and the reptiles would wake to vicious life again. But winter was far away.

Thola, drifting into sleep, dreamed of the fierce black snake whose bite was death and cried in distress and the king bent over her and soothed her.

15

ALTOGETHER about five hundred women died, but now not even death was a deterrent. The sly whispers continued and the people, when they passed Thola, lowered their eyes; in the isigodlo the women avoided her; the sister of Umbopha averted her head and smiled secretly.

Thola endured her ostracism in silent misery. The knowledge that she had brought such a plight on herself acted as a persistent goad: she had, after all, given UmuSa a charm made from scrapings obtained from the king's body; she had spoken out against the king, not once but many times, and survived; what could the people think other than that she was a powerful witch? No other human being had ever wielded power over the Black One of the AmaZulu; his mother, perhaps, to a slight degree, but even his mother had never criticised him openly nor had she truly influenced his indomitable will. There was the story that she had once attempted to save the live of a new-born child of Tshaka's; rumour murmured that Nandi had been banished from the king's presence; some had it that the king had even assaulted his mother in his tremendous anger, but this Thola did not believe. The child, certainly, had been destroyed.

As the old saying goes, she told herself, I must hold my tongue, and she walked glumly down to the river where the women gathered for their morning ablutions. A cool wind scudded across the water and pale sunlight filtered through clouds that were darkening the sky and banking sullenly against the horizon in the direction of the sea. Dead leaves swept by in the eddying twists of the river and disappeared around the bend; Thola watched the leaves sombrely, feeling just as helpless, as if she too were being swept away by the outgoing water in a swift journey towards regions as unknown as the mysterious sea.

Ostentatiously the women turned away from her and began to croon a soft dirge-like refrain; one or two of Tshaka's favoured ones preened themselves, and now and again the pale sunlight fell upon their brass collars and arm-bands and struck fiery sparks of gold. Slyly they looked around, drawing in the other women; the ranks closed and glistening black bodies grouped tightly around the place where it was easiest to bathe. Thola moved forward but the women would not permit her amongst them. She felt her temper rising and controlled herself with difficulty. She could, of course, bathe farther down but the river was tricky, shallow in one spot and too deep in another and she was not yet familiar with its artifices; if she misjudged the depth and disappeared beneath the water the ignominy of having to call for help would surely provoke her to screaming fury, and then – and then she might again say too much.

She pulled herself up straight and tall and looked contemptuously at pronounced buttocks and swelling bellies: simpletons, savages, cows, too bovine for words, empty-headed, fools who believed . . .

A giggle disturbed her thoughts; glances darted at her and away again.

'The Black One allows no one to use the medicines of love,' a woman muttered. 'The Black One punishes those who attempt to use love medicines in secret.'

Her sisters murmured their agreement.

'My God,' thought Thola, 'do they really imagine

that I poison Tshaka with aphrodisiacs?' Her temper flamed.

'What is that?' she screeched. 'What did you say? You will say that to the king!'

'No word passed my lips,' a woman whispered and gave a little, stupid titter. 'Did I say a word, my sisters?'

'Not a word passed your lips,' her companions said, grinning slyly. 'Not a word. We will bear witness for you.'

'Let me through,' Thola said and walked determinedly forward. 'Let me through at once. I wish to bathe.'

'Withering flowers need water,' a girl remarked; and again the women formed into a circle and turned their backs on Thola. 'When the flower is sere we will tear the petals off one by one.'

'My flower,' Thola heard Tshaka's voice say lingeringly, and the breath caught in her throat; and again, 'Cause no more trouble,' and she beat down her anger and turned away from the women and found a cool spot beneath a tree and waited for them to finish with their splashing and laughing. They took their time, screaming shrilly and throwing little barbs at her; but at last they trooped back to the kraal, and then she walked down to the water's edge and bathed.

On her way back to the kraal a snake hissed beneath her feet and its darting, triangular head just missed her ankle and she leaped wildly and ran in terror and arrived at her hut breathless and sick with fear. Immediately she saw that no food had been left for her; and on her platter was an impaled cockroach; the women had never been able to understand her revulsion for these insects and had mocked when she had scrubbed her meat platter instead of leaving it to be cleaned in the orthodox way. With the slight chill in the air and her strenuous exertions, her appetite was keen, and by midday the hollowness in the pit of her stomach was like a pain. She had become conditioned to eating only two meals a day but now sundown, the time of the next meal, seemed centuries away.

Wait, she promised herself grimly, just wait until I get to the king. And then the vision of strewn corpses and silly faces stilled in death obtruded upon her. If she told the king the women would surely die, not for her sake alone but because Tshaka could not afford dissension and spite, particularly if it were directed against one whom he so openly favoured. It would be a great wickedness if these stupid women died because of her own past indiscretions: honesty compelled her to admit that she alone was responsible for her present predicament. In the beginning the women had been prepared to be friendly; she had not queened it over them, certainly, but tact had been wanting. And there was UmuSa, as potent a force in the isigodlo as if she were still vibrantly alive.

At the start of the evening meal there was a flurried scramble for the cooking-pots and, with deliberate intent, Thola was shouldered out of the way; hunger spurred her on to greater effort and she managed to snatch a small piece of meat, which she wolfed down. Later she suffered from an acute attack of indigestion and was listless; even in the king's presence she was apathetic.

After several days of such victimisation at the hands of the harem women she was ready to weep with despair. Where, formerly, she had not given the thought of food much attention she now dwelt longingly on recollections of previous meals; existence had become divided into two great moments of utmost importance: the hour of food in the morning and the hour of food at night. The vibrancy had gone out of her step and she stooped her shoulders as if to subdue the ache of hunger in her stomach; she was easily wearied and slept badly and failed to be an entertaining companion for Tshaka. Had there been some solution other than that of telling the king how she was being treated life would still have seemed tolerable; but the knowledge that her complaints would bring death distressed her even more than the physical pain caused by hunger.

She reckoned that in a week she had eaten less than she normally ate in a day, and yearned for a friend whom she could consult, someone to whom she could turn in her trouble. She had no one but Tshaka and to him she could not go.

Then he noticed her pallor and exhaustion. She was sitting beside him in his hut and had sunk forward to ease the pain in her belly. As always she was aware of his nearness but the familiar excitement did not shake her; instead, for the very first time she was really and truly afraid of him; and not only of him but of his people as well. If women were so cruel she shuddered to think what treatment vengeful men would offer someone they wished out of the way. She remembered the woman who had been barricaded in her hut and left to starve and shivered violently.

Suddenly Tshaka commanded 'Bring light,' and he jerked the flaming rush from the servant and lifted Thola's chin and held the rush near her face. She kept her eyes lowered and vainly attempted to raise the drooping corners of her mouth, but her lips would not smile. Dimly she heard the other women crooning in their corner and the soft refrain held accents of intimidation.

'You are ill, my flower,' Tshaka observed, his voice deep with concern.

'No, Lord,' she whispered, and a nerve in her cheek twitched spasmodically.

'Come,' the king said, handing the rush back to the

waiting servant, 'something is wrong. You had better tell me.'

She welcomed the half-darkness which came as soon as the servant withdrew; the women's singing stopped and the profound stillness allowed her to hear her own weary breathing.

'Nothing, Lord. Nothing,' she whimpered.

Alertly Tshaka looked towards the quiet women; they sat so still, their crooning silenced, even their breathing muted. He called out a name and a girl crept forward reluctantly.

'What ails your sister?' he asked.

The girl began to tremble.

'Answer,' Tshaka ordered.

'Lord of Blackness, she has been unable to eat.'

'Is that so?' Tshaka said, his eyes flicking over the girl.

'That is so,' the girl sighed.

'Fetch an emetic,' Tshaka commanded. 'Immediately.'

Which, Thola reflected tiredly and bitterly, is considered an infallible remedy; and she saw herself vomiting uncontrollably in Tshaka's presence. He would not find such an occurrence distasteful but that knowledge did not help her. She had had her share of humiliation. Besides she was not sure that she would survive the violent emetic commonly used.

'As you say, Lord,' the girl said and made a grave mistake by shooting a triumphant look at Thola; and the breathing in the corner became easier, held perhaps a cadence of exultation too.

'An emetic will be of no use,' Thola said, her eyelids leaping up and her eyes sparking, and energy born of anger ran like waves through her, so that she held herself as of old, shoulder-straight; and her habitual air of haughtiness returned, and pride; and she looked at the girl as if she considered spurning her with a contemptuous foot. 'An emetic will most likely kill me and then your – your "sisters" – will realise their ambition anyway.'

Tshaka smiled lazily and gently. 'How so?'

'They will not let me eat,' Thola said. 'They are trying to starve me to death. The fools – as if I am afraid of them. They will not let me use the bathing-place. They do not speak to me, which is no hardship for I do not suffer fools gladly. They are stupid...'

'Thola,' said the king warningly.

'They say I give you medicines of love,' Thola hurried on, words tumbling out, and her very weakness filled her voice with greater venom, for now she wanted to break down and weep and had to force the cutting hardness into her voice. 'They think I have bewitched you. They say I am a witch!'

In the shadows the women sat frozen; the girl Tshaka had summoned was grovelling at his feet.

'Indeed?' the king said. 'There is a plague of women in this land. Come forward,' and he waited while the women crept nearer. Death hovered above them. 'Go and fetch food for my sister. Be careful in your selection. Be quick. And say not one word to anyone, for if you do, within this hour your tongue will be silenced for always.'

He sat back, the shadows claiming his face; moment after moment passed; minutes lengthened intolerably.

'Lord, permit me to eat alone in my hut,' Thola begged. 'I do not know what effect food will have upon me.'

'They shall feed you,' Tshaka said, 'on their knees.'

'Ah, no,' her cry of protest echoed in the hut. 'That would be a punishment for me. I shall perhaps not be able to keep down the food. They have humiliated me enough.'

'Be still, small one,' the king commanded.

When a girl returned with a platter heaped with choice meat he sent her off again, commanding her to bring amasi and beer. With his own fingers he took a small piece of meat and broke it into fragments.

'Hold out your hands,' he said to Thola; obediently she brought her palms together.

'Dogs,' Tshaka said to the women, 'take a fragment each and offer it to this woman and plead with her for your lives.'

Nausea came at the odour of the meat and Thola scarcely heard the women but the king listened grimly to every word. When the girl returned with the sour milk and the beer she too was commanded to kneel before Thola.

'Return now to your quarters,' the king said. 'If any of you dare to discuss what has taken place my ears shall hear your words and you shall die slowly and in great suffering. Go!'

Then he ordered a servant to bring water and took the fragments of meat out of Thola's cupped hands and gave these to the servant; and he himself washed her hands for her.

'The smell of meat sickens you,' he observed. 'There is goodness in the amasi,' and he picked up the container and fed her gently; and afterwards made her drink of the beer; and warmth came and the nausea subsided. She wanted more, begged for more, but he told the servant to remove the utensils and the food.

'Later,' he said. 'Do not burden your body with too much at once. My flower, you kept all this from me.'

'I did not want to be the cause of death,' Thola cried, and remembered UmuSa and shuddered.

'Come, now you must rest. Later in the night I shall wake you and you shall have more food; and tomorrow too, at intervals, until you are strong again and can take food in the normal way.' He cradled her to him and put the palm of his hand under her cheek, as if to provide a pillow; with his other hand he stroked her forehead soothingly and she drifted into a deep sleep. Again and again during the night he woke her and fed her and afterwards soothed her back to sleep; when the dawn came he sent her back to her hut; the women greeted her humbly and made way for her, but hatred emanated from them as if it were a living thing.

At the river they parted for her when she went to bathe and saluted her as if she were a queen, and she was more alone than ever before.

Tshaka waited until she had quite recovered and then he said, his voice impersonal, 'You have become a source of great danger to me.'

And she knew that this was true.

'That tongue of yours,' he added reflectively, 'and your flagrant disobedience. Who would have believed that a woman would threaten Tshaka's might?'

'I called those women stupid,' Thola muttered, 'but I am – and have been – even more stupid. What can I do, Lord?'

'Nothing. It is too late, my flower. You make me seem weak, which I am not, but the sight of my people is not always keen. I have been thinking that I shall have to send you away.'

'Away!' The future became bleak and arid.

'For your own safety, Thola. And for mine. If the people think a woman can rule me they will become restless. I am not blind to the fact that there is a dangerous element, an envious one, among them. And now even the women imagine they can defy me.'

'They are jealous – and very silly,' Thola remarked wanly.

'That may be,' the king said sombrely, 'but the danger is not lessened. I have in mind to send you to

Fynn. With him you will be safe. But you will be with those who sought his protection and it will be necessary for you to guard your tongue carefully.'

'Must I go, Lord? Will you send me away soon?'

'Soon enough,' Tshaka said and sighed; and she saw that he was weary and that, for once, he looked his age. 'I have also heard rumours concerning the boy who brought you to me.'

Thola looked up in quick alarm and then avoided the king's intent eyes.

'That troubles you,' he said.

'Only because he is – or was – a friend and tried to save my life at the cost of his own. What are the rumours, Lord?'

'That he casts spells.'

At that she laughed. 'Malanga could not do that. He is terrified of anything to do with witchcraft. He found courage but not wisdom, Lord. He is sometimes very much a fool.'

'I do not want you to be over-concerned for this boy's safety.'

'I am not. No one could ever prove that he had anything to do with spells.'

'No proof is required,' the king said and smiled gently. 'When you go to Fynn I shall see that this boy is sent off in the opposite direction.'

'Do that, Lord, if it pleases you.'

He appeared not to hear her; he was staring before him, clenching and unclenching his hands, and she watched the powerful rippling of muscles along his arms; then, as if he had reached a decision, he relaxed against the skins and the gentle smile came to his lips.

'Thola,' he said, 'before the end of spring you shall be with Fynn. Until then I think you may safely remain here. But there is a darkness in the air. I can sense it. Should anything happen to me – anything at all which may affect my authority – I want you to leave for Fynn's settlement immediately. Do you understand that?'

'Do you mean if you should be in danger? I would not leave you then!'

'Now be quiet and listen to me. I order you to go to Fynn at the slightest sign of trouble. Do you hear me?'

'I would not leave you,' Thola cried passionately. 'I might as well be dead as to have to live without you.'

'Those are fine words. I think you mean them. Do you?'

She crouched over his knees, bending her head; and she was cold and terribly afraid.

'Sit up,' the king said. 'Look at me. You will give me your word that you will go.'

'I will not. I will not.' If he expected her to weep he was disappointed. Terror at the thought of harm to him burned away all tears.

'You defy me,' the king said evenly.

'I defy you,' she whispered, her jaw set in such a stubborn line that momentarily she bore a remarkable physical likeness to Tshaka. 'Nothing would make me leave you. Do you hear me? Nothing. Nothing!'

'I do not like women's voices when they are raised in high-pitched screams,' Tshaka said; it seemed as if he were torn between laughter and anger, and then laughter triumphed. 'You are weary of life then,' he teased.

'You know that is not true. You sit there and mock me; but you know I could not live without you.'

'I do not mock you, my flower,' the king said, sombreness returning. 'You are too close to my heart for mockery. Perhaps if I did not bring lightness to my words I would weep like a foolish woman.' With great gentleness he cradled her against him. 'I want you to be ready to depart to Fynn's settlement – be ready today –

185

tomorrow – and every day after that. When the moment comes that it is absolutely necessary to show my people – particularly the murmurers – that Tshaka rules this country, I want you in safety. Thola . . .' – his hand slipped along her shoulders and caressed and she knew that he was hardly aware of her or of what he was doing; yet, despite this knowledge, his nearness was like a soporific and numbed her brain.

'Lord?'

'My nights have been plagued by unpleasant dreams. I am not afraid of omens and, as a rule, I am not dictated to by dreams and fears of witchcraft, but . . .'

She heard the deepness of his voice but not his words.

'There was a time,' she said, breath catching in her throat, 'when you would not even touch me. When you were fearful of touching me . . .'

His sudden stillness alarmed her; and then he pressed her against him and she thought wildly and exultantly, 'Good God! He is weeping. He is weeping because of me!' and tears came spilling into her eyes, and she looked up into his face; and she saw that the king was shaking with voiceless laughter; and presently the laughter echoed through the hut; indeed there were tears in his eyes, but they were tears of mirth.

'I was right,' she muttered suspiciously, 'you do mock me.'

'Oh you,' he laughed, 'you with your bright mind. You are just a woman. What now, my flower? What do you want me to do? Say that you have conquered me?'

'I wish I could. I would die for you but just now I should like to . . . I should like to . . .'

'What, dear one? Make me grovel?'

'Make you grovel. Yes, I should like to have that happen.'

'And then you would be disappointed. You would say to yourself, "Is this my king? This weakling who is on his knees to me? I was mistaken in Tshaka." Would you not?'

At least he had not pushed her away from him and she forgave him and snuggled closer and began to share his merriment.

'I expect you are right,' she agreed. 'But I wish I could have got the better of you just once.'

'You have, my flower. Many times. You are alive and you should be in the land of the spirits.'

'Should I, Lord? Have I deserved that?'

'Over and over again. Even now I am keeping you here – against my better judgment. You should leave for Fynn tonight – but tomorrow you will still be here. And perhaps even for many months to come. Say in truth to yourself that you have succeeded where all others have failed. You have conquered Tshaka.'

He did not send her away but left her to fall asleep on the skins near him; and he did not call other women to him, which was, for her, a deep delight.

Late in the night she awoke and heard the king moaning in his sleep; raising herself she saw that his face was drawn into a grimace and that drops of sweat shone on his forehead; she called his name softly and he twisted away from her and suddenly threshed out with his arms, striking her against her chin; she fell forward and in that instant he was awake and alert and called urgently: 'Thola!'

His face blurred and, in the firelight, he seemed to be stained in crimson blood; without thinking she cried, 'You are wet with blood! What is it? What is it?'

He passed a hand over his face and looked down at the palm.

'There is nothing,' he said, and his oriental eyes narrowed.

'I must have been dreaming,' but she drew away, for the illusion persisted; and suddenly she thought, 'How does a man feel when he knows that he has shed the blood of thousands? What I see is not real but what he has done is real. Can a country be worth so great a sacrifice?' The horror continued to grow; it was as if all the blood of all those Tshaka had done to death was pouring over him; and the hut was massed with voiceless forms; and outside the Royal hut and all over the quiet land more ghosts pressed.

'There is no blood,' the king said again, wonderingly.

'No, Lord. A dream has no substance,' and she shivered violently.

'What did you dream?'

'I do not know,' and she shook her head with unnecessary violence. 'I have forgotten. You were also dreaming, Lord. You moaned in your sleep and you struck me,' and she rubbed at her chin.

'That is so.' Alertly the black eyes flicked over her and the grim lines of the king's lips softened. 'You dream of blood. Perhaps that is good, Thola. You have made up my mind for me. It is better not to put off what must be done.'

'Lord?'

For a moment he unbent. 'Did I hurt you?'

'No, Lord. What is it that you must do?'

'Tomorrow,' the king said, 'I shall call together the diviners; and messages will go out to all my people to gather here. The guilty ones will be discovered.'

'There are no guilty ones. Of witchcraft, I mean. But I will be denounced. And Malanga.'

'You,' said the king gravely, 'will not be here.'

'And Malanga?'

'And Malanga?' Tshaka mocked.

'Lord,' and she bent towards him, but he pushed her impatiently.

'Go to your hut now,' he ordered. 'Trouble me not.'

She saw that words would be futile and she crept out

of the hut and into the darkness and past the guards; and then slipped into the shadows and sat quietly behind the king's hut and her mind darted into the future and the future was dark and horrible.

16

At this time Dingane and Mhlangana, Tshaka's half-brothers, were at Dukuza; and often they were in the company of Umbopha, Tshaka's trusted servant. Thola had not seen a great deal of the two brothers but the few glimpses she had caught of them had not impressed her. They were unquestionably of the Royal house but Thola could not help but feel that a superficial physical likeness was the only genuine link they had with the Zulu king. On the other hand, Tshaka's personality was such that the bravest and most powerful of his warriors became nonentities in his presence.

Now, crouching in the darkness, Thola thought of the two brothers and, surrendering to an impulse, crept towards Umbopha's quarters. Scrawny dogs sniffed around her and one near-savage monster barked ferociously, but she was not attacked for she had the smell of the kraal about her; presently the dogs tired of her and curled up their gaunt frames and sleep came to them and relieved them of the gnawing unease caused by hunger.

And then three figures emerged from a large central hut; firelight shone out from the small opening at the front of the hut and shed a red radiance upon the looming shadows and Thola recognised Dingane, and then Mhlangana; behind the brothers walked Umbopha. As always, a look of sly wisdom was upon his features.

Stirred now by an intuitive warning, Thola crept after the men, her movements as stealthy as those of the men; and she heard a whispered allusion to Tshaka, and that whisper held a threat of death; and she knew that if the three conspirators discovered her, death would indeed be *her* portion; an exceedingly quiet death: the strangling grip of strong fingers or the sudden twisting of her neck.

The need to warm the king became so urgent that a recklessness invaded her and she almost turned and ran for the Royal hut; a twig snapped beneath her feet and the men became silent statues; she too waited, motionless, in the black night, and her blood made a frightened tumult in her ears, and it seemed strange that she alone could hear this frenzied sound.

Minutes passed and then a sigh from one of the men dropped into the terrible silence; another whispered, 'It is nothing,' and quietly they continued their slow, careful walk.

For a long while Thola, fearing a trap and not daring to move, stood quite still. Beneath the trees, a little distance away, the darkness was so intense that she could discern no movement, yet she had received the impression that the men had walked in the direction of the grove. She herself was engulfed in darkness and she did not know whether she could be seen; an unmoving shadow somehow adopts the lineaments of a tree or bush, but movement, she knew, immediately betrays shape and form.

She had not known that such weariness could come from standing in one position; her back began to ache and sudden cramp pulled in the muscles of her calves; and then a swaying seemed to take hold of her body and a faintness broke in soft, lapping waves over her, and her endurance came to an end. She fell to her knees and managed to retain that position for a while; no sudden footfalls came to disturb the quietude and cautiously, cautiously, she edged back towards Tshaka's hut. When she reached it, she thought confusedly she would scream out his name; the king's brothers would not reach her in time to kill her for the guards would protect her.

The guards. Perhaps they were in the plot; it would be easy for them to club her down, to remove her corpse secretly, to arrange matters so that it would seem that a wild animal had attacked her and savaged her to death.

She paused, came to a decision, skirted Tshaka's quarters and crept quietly along and into her sleeping hut; and all through the night she sat on her mat, keeping an attentive vigil, alert for the slightest alien noise, and all those hours were filled with the thought that at first light the king must be warned.

'Sekusile,' she told herself, 'it has dawned,' and then she knew that she would not move off her sleeping mat; and she knew that she would not warn Tshaka; she thought of the day he had gone to war, marching with his warriors, the dust clouds flying and the triumphant song of war rolling out in his deep bass voice, and she remembered how she had agonised, 'if he should die . . . if *he* should die . . .'; and she cowered down on her mat and wept. Now he would surely die.

If she warned Tshaka of the plot against him he would remove Dingane and Mhlangana, and Umbopha would die a terrible death; then the king would call the nation together and the witch hunt would take place, that smelling-out he had decided upon.

She would be safe with Fynn, and many hundreds of innocent people would be murdered because a woman called Thola had come into the life of the Zulu king. She could confess to Tshaka; she could tell him about UmuSa. But that would make no difference. For her betrayal the king would undoubtedly kill her but so many would die with her.

A thousand – or one man? That one man Tshaka. And she could not bear to think of him and bitter pain burned up her tears.

No possibility existed that he would deal with Dingane and Mhlangana and Umbopha only; if Tshaka could not point to other conspirators he would contrive such traitors, for it would be necessary for him to impress the people with his strength and merciless- ness; the vultures would fatten on the corpses of his people; through many days the evil birds would gorge themselves.

When the morning light grew brighter Thola rose tiredly from her sleeping mat and went out into the early morning air; already cooking fires were sending up smoke to scent the wind with a pleasantly acrid tang; and the wind held a slight chill for it blew out- wards from the sea and inland. Thola paused on a little prominence and stared down at the far distant sea and wished that she had drowned that day long ago when the slaver went below the green waters.

The thought of food nauseated her and she avoided the cooking-pots and walked down to the river, a tiny, solitary figure, and bathed and felt no cleaner. Pre- sently other women came down and bathed and filled their water-pots; as usual the women crooned little songs and giggled and teased; and it seemed strange to Thola that they could be so happy and laugh with such joyous irresponsibility; and stranger that the sky was a pellucid blue and the sun warm in its shining splendour.

The awful day passed slowly and nothing happened and towards evening she had convinced herself that the plot to kill the king had been abandoned; a day had come to its end.

After nightfall the king sent for her; he seemed deeply preoccupied with his own thoughts and did not speak for a long time; when at last he turned to her she was infinitely distressed by the sadness which lay like a dark mantle over him; his eyes were opaque and expressionless and no laughter wrinkles creased up towards his temples. A gnawing pain lodged in her throat and her lips began to tremble. Surely he was too young to die; at the most he could not be more than forty.

'Four days after tomorrow my messengers will be leaving to call together the nation,' Tshaka said. 'You will also leave. You will be escorted to Fynn. He will care for you.'

This time she did not plead with him.

'I will go to Fynn, Lord,' she whispered, 'if you wish.'

The king's glance sharpened. 'You are not often so obedient,' he said.

'Words are futile, Lord. I know I cannot bend your will. And I have brought you enough trouble.' To escape his eyes she bent her head but she did not weep. 'Will I see you again?' she asked wanly.

'Do not be so sad,' the king said. 'Do not be too sad.'

She had tears left, after all, and they trickled down her cheeks and she did not wipe them away. The king made no reply, as if he knew that she had put the question more to herself than to him.

'When your people answer your summons and gather here many will die,' she said.

'Many will die,' Tshaka agreed gravely.

'Do not die, Lord,' she said, her voice so low he hardly heard her. 'Do not die.'

Very faintly the laughter wrinkles fanned out around his eyes; he put out a hand and gently touched her chin.

'Let me boast and say my name will live forever,' the king said.

'Forever, Lord. Forever.' Haltingly she began to talk to Tshaka, driven by the need to justify herself. 'I am not like you, Lord,' she said. 'I cannot feel that people are expendable. I cannot bear to think that many

194

should suffer for a vague, ultimate good. One man, I think, is of as much importance as a thousand men. I wish with all my heart that you were just an ordinary man – a member of the humble Thuli tribe – living under Fynn's protection. A speck of dust. But you are Tshaka Zulu. The AmaZulu are fierce and proud and you are the fiercest and proudest of all.'

'The day will come – is almost here – when every tribe will forget its clan name. Not a man but he will say he is a Zulu – a child of heaven,' Tshaka said.

'And then, Lord?'

'And then, my flower?' Tshaka said and smiled.

Thola watched him take snuff and her nose wrinkled and the laughter wrinkles around his eyes deepened and spread and spread.

'You do not even sneeze,' she observed, and the ache in her throat increased; now at the hour of parting she could find nothing better to discuss than trivialities; now when she wanted to fling herself at his feet and weep out her agony she had to sit at a distance and force her lips into a grimace of a smile. 'Once, long ago, I sneezed. You were very angry.'

'Angry,' Tshaka said. 'Angry, my flower?'

'Ah, Lord,' she whispered, and her mouth quivered and she gripped her hands together and held them steady in her lap.

'You must go now,' Tshaka said, and he moved back and she knew that he would not touch her again. 'Tomorrow we shall see each other only from a distance and tomorrow night I shall not call you. Soon enough after that you will be on your way to Fynn.'

'Do not forget me, Lord,' she said.

'I will remember you, Thola.'

'Must I go now, Lord? Now?'

'Go now, Thola.'

'My father,' she said submissively, and in her ears

came the moaning of great winds; and like rain her tears fell. 'Sala gahle, Lord,' she cried. 'Stay well.'

'Hamba gahle, my flower,' Tshaka said, and turned his head away. 'Go well, Thola.'

The guard stepped aside for her and outside the hut was a world of emptiness, and secret shadows and wraithlike mists; and she thought she could hear the ominous pounding of the sea, but that was not so, for the sea was far away. The strong September winds howled in the trees and the sound of this howling was a sadness.

Silence lay upon the huge kraal and she said her farewell to Dukuza; indeed in that place she had lost her way.

The isigodlo women were all asleep, but for Thola there was no rest; she lay upon her mat and again waited for the dawn; and it was very long in coming.

She did not know how death would come to the king, or when. A club perhaps? Not strangling fingers; no man was strong enough to hold Tshaka down. Now, this moment, the king might be dead; if not, then with the dawn; if not with the dawn of light, then in the heat of the day or the cool dusk of evening. Perhaps in the black, silent hours of night. But death would surely come and at a moment when Tshaka least expected treachery. He who had wished to be honourably left behind in battle would be struck down by a traitor.

Again she gripped her hands together and they were wet with sweat. Traitor's hands. And her heart cried desperately, 'Lord! Lord!', and the silence reproached her.

How could it be that the king who through all the years had appeared invulnerable, should now be exposed to certain death? He gave no indication that he was aware of a definite plot; perhaps he knew and was biding his time. But Tshaka always acted swiftly; and as much as he protested against the taking of action where such action would involve the 'children of his father', without a doubt he would remove Dingane and Mhlangana were he convinced that they were traitors.

How she would welcome death, Thola reflected, if in the morning Tshaka suddenly revealed that he knew of her disloyalty; if he summarily dismissed Dingane and Mhlangana and Umbopha and ordered their execution.

But, within herself, she felt that that would not happen; the awful web of fate had enmeshed the king within its intricacies; for him there was no escape.

17

On a dull September morning in 1828, Tshaka dreamed of death; he awoke from the dream of sadness and told those in attendance; one of the women who was amongst those in whom he had confided his dream could not still her lips. Omens and terrible portents were discovered. Already there was a rumour about that a smelling-out ceremony was to take place before the winds presaging the intense heat of summer had blown themselves out. Already many wore a sullen look upon their faces and kept their eyes downcast: Dukuza had become a place of foreboding.

When Umbopha heard of the king's dream he went immediately to Dingane and Mhlangana and said to them: 'We can delay no longer.'

Dingane and Mhlangana, who were not men of the stature of Tshaka, trembled and grew afraid, and murmured in their cowardice: 'We need time to think. Our plan must not miscarry. We must have time. That is so.'

'There is no time,' Umbopha told them, and his mouth set in a hard line and his eyes glittered. 'Today the Great Elephant will be no more. You know that he plans to do away with his enemies. No one knows who will be plucked out by the soothsayers, the diviners. The Black One is a king of great cleverness. Be sure that the guilty ones will be those who conspire against him.'

'He will never turn his spear against us,' Mhlangana muttered, half turning away, remembering perhaps that Tshaka had always protected the children of Senzangakhona.

'Even those who love him turn against him now and say that he is shedding too much blood,' Dingane said, and his eyes also glittered; and the dark shadows of hideous cruelties fell upon the land of the Zulu people.

'That is true. These days he eats up the members of his own body. No one is secure,' Umbopha whispered, and he drew closer to the brothers. 'You may listen, for I speak truly. Even you are not secure. The vultures wheel hungrily over your heads. You will die if the Black One continues to live. The Black One must die.'

The brothers stood in silence for a long while; they drew upon their courage; they agreed.

'I will be your eyes,' Umbopha said. 'I will watch and when the moment arrives I will give you a signal. Therefore remain as close to the king as you can. My signal will be the throwing of my stick. Keep your hands steady; strike swiftly and surely. Any delay will cost you your lives.'

And the three men went their several ways.

As was his wont, the king bathed before his people; the wind, gathering strength, howled about him; the wan sunlight touched him pallidly. Apart from adulatory murmurs, the concourse watched and waited in oppressive silence; yet it was a day of clemency, for no one died. Who could say what it was that brought a dryness to the throat and a sense of disaster to the heart?

Once Tshaka smiled swiftly at one of his counsellors, and Thola almost called out in pain; the smile irradiated the king's features; the laughter wrinkles fanned out, but the deep bass laughter did not complement the smile; as on the people, so on the king lay a sorrowful depression of spirits.

For Thola the anguish of the moment was unbearable; Tshaka was still alive and mighty in his strength;

she could still go to him and say: 'Lord, this man, Umbopha, conspires against you; he seeks your life; Dingane and Mhlangana conspire with him. Believe me, I heard their words with my own ears. Your brothers seek to kill you. Forget now that they are also the children of your father and slay them.'

But she did not move; stood dully and watched the king. Drops of water glistened on his broad chest; he turned his head and his powerful profile was momentarily etched against sombre light.

Someone moaned in awe and a deep sigh swept through the gathering.

And Thola thought: 'If the king's brother were here, if Ngwadi were here, Tshaka would not be in danger of death. Ngwadi loves him as Nandi loved him; for the king's sake, Ngwadi would hold an impi at bay; dead bodies would pile up in a pyramid before assailants could reach Tshaka; Ngwadi would give up his life for his brother.'

She shuddered; she too would give up her life for the king. But not the lives of thousands of innocents. And yet, would not those innocents die gladly for the king? Did not his warriors promise that if the king fell in battle their bodies would cover him? To the last man they would stand and fight. 'Sigidi!' that great war cry would echo around them, and many among the foe would accompany them to the land of spirits. 'Sigidi!' they would shout, and 'Sesidlile!– We have eaten!'

Sigidi.

He who is the equal of a thousand.

Unequalled, Thola thought brokenly, and dropped her head.

Now Tshaka was walking towards the seat of council. 'Bayete!' the people exclaimed. The bird plumes swayed above the king's head; the wind came in great gusts and the bird plumes bowed before the wind; the king's cloak flared out behind him, and he walked slowly and heavily.

Unexpectedly power came to the sun, and the heat increased until sweat dewed every face; strangely the wind quietened and soon dark clouds began to crouch along the horizon; as noon approached shadows darkened; a breathless stillness touched upon Dukuza.

Far away the waters of the sea grew grey as the clouds overhead shut out the light; the great waves slowly relinquished their crashing surges; the breakers softened into mere heaving swells; the seabirds called sadly. Many miles out lightning blazed above the dun-coloured water.

The king retired to his hut and left himself unguarded. This Thola saw. Often he fretted against having guards posted around the Royal hut and this was such a day.

'Now? Will it come now?' she asked herself, lingering close by, taut with expectancy. But no one ventured near. Despair enveloped her. Not yet, but soon. And she forced herself to walk unconcernedly to the huts of the women, the king's sisters.

There she encountered the usual chatter, the irresponsible attitude to life, the brittle childishness; and yet, now and again, a sudden gravity; an untoward seriousness.

'It is an evil dream,' one woman said authoritatively, 'there is evil brewing. The Black One's dream fills me with foreboding.'

If these women could read her thoughts, what would they do to her, Thola wondered. Fall upon her and tear her living body to pieces? Perhaps the sister of Umbopha would greet her as a friend; undoubtedly the sister of Umbopha would embrace her and call her a great and wise friend.

If the king died would a number of these women have

to accompany him to the land of spirits? Would he be given the burial befitting a king? How would his brothers deal with his body? Would a regiment stand guard? Would the people forget his splendour, his brilliance, his extraordinary power of mind, and remember his cruelties? Was it possible that she could sit with the chattering women and calmly reflect on the king's death?

Perhaps she would be one of those who would be chosen to follow him into the valley of the shadow of death. That did not disturb her, nor was there comfort to be found. A deadness of feeling weighed her down, worse somehow than the heartache which had preceded it.

'That was the time a dog climbed up onto the roof of a hut,' she heard a woman saying. 'What evil things happened. Sadness came to all of us.'

A chorus of distressed sounds issued from the other women; but one girl, so young, certainly one of Tshaka's favourites, twisted a brass band which she wore around her arm, and preened herself and thought perhaps of future happiness when the king would summon her to him.

If Umbopha's plot succeeded, there would be no summoning; for Thola, whatever happened, there would be no reunion. If the king escaped death, life with Fynn awaited her. Fynn was known as a man of great kindness and the people under his protection worshipped him. Yet – nothing was of any consequence. She could envisage herself enslaved again; the idea did not even stir her.

The women's talk had now turned to beadwork, but Thola hardly heard the discussion. Presently the misdeeds of a woman caught in adultery were deliberated upon; the woman had died, as had her lover. The magpie chatter drifted on to marriage.

'The Great Elephant will release two regiments,' the vain young girl maintained. 'A male regiment and a female regiment. Then we will have much feasting,' and she sighed, thinking perhaps of the children she would never have; but soon enough she brightened again. 'Feasting and dancing,' she said.

Thola could have told her that there would be neither feasting nor dancing. Only sorrow. Surely many would be sad at the king's death. Surely his warriors would weep like women; his people would despair.

All at once she could not bear the presence of the women any longer; she sidled away and, driven by an urgent need to escape the environs of the kraal, almost ran down to the river, so often a refuge for her. Everywhere was that heavy silence; not a blade of grass stirred, and the water of the river was ashen grey and seemed scarcely to move.

The silence, the heaviness, was not somnolent; rather, in the hush danger lurked. Stillness should bring a feeling of peace, of sleepy content; this stillness held within it a grave apprehension: that sense of terror when one waits, breathing repressed, for a nameless horror to reveal itself.

And Thola looked up at Dukuza, the Royal kraal: an enormous circle of huts, the Royal hut prominent because of its size; and her eyes wandered over the cattle enclosures, the women's huts, and the lethargically moving figures of the people.

None of the usual hustle and bustle was evident; but now and again a dog barked warningly.

Of course an approaching storm always affected the people adversely. The nagging fear that lightning would strike a hut – which often happened – was always present. When lightning struck and killed, death was not mentioned; whoever died had been called home by the spirits. The hut in which the fatality occurred was left and it gradually crumbled into a ruin beneath the onslaught of wind and rain.

Suddenly a voice called a greeting and Thola looked up; men were crossing the ford at the river; strangers they were, that was obvious, perhaps come from Fynn, perhaps those whom Tshaka had requested Fynn to direct to Dukuza. If they were indeed from Fynn she knew that before two sunrises they would be taking her back with them to the settlement at the bay.

She dreaded being away from Dukuza; she dreaded not knowing whether Tshaka was alive or dead. Her thoughts seemed callous, but that was not the way with her: heartbreak could not have been deeper.

'You sit here alone, woman,' one of the strangers called teasingly.

'I am weary,' she replied, and managed to smile. 'Are you from Sofili? From Fynn?'

'That we are not,' the man returned; already he and the others were on their way to the Royal kraal, but he continued to converse, in the way of the people, by shouting as he walked. 'We bring treasures for the Great One. Feathers and fine skins.'

'You are delayed, I think,' Thola shouted back, much relieved. 'You have been expected for many days.'

'We came as swiftly as we could,' the man yelled; after that the distance became too great and further speech was impossible.

Thola watched the figures of the men; smaller and smaller they grew, and at last vanished into the kraal. Tshaka would not wear the fine skins; the brilliant feathers would never form a decoration for him.

Far away thunder growled. Somehow the water in the river seemed to be gathering strength and running with greater speed; little whorls formed and carried leaves forward in tiny, advancing circles; and Thola remembered how she had explained to Malanga that she had been washed ashore from the wrecked slaver the way a leaf is swept up against a river bank.

That vignette from the remote past seemed a dream and her days as a slave the imaginings of a warped brain; nothing now had reality except the king and his approaching doom. Endurance was wearing thin; without consciously admitting it to herself she was dimly aware that unless events moved quickly she would sacrifice Malanga; she would sacrifice all the innocent ones. She would run to Tshaka and throw herself before him and reveal to him all that she knew. And at that moment, without conscious decision, she jumped to her feet and tried to run, but her legs had become numb because they had been modestly tucked beneath her for the hours she had been sitting on the river bank. She fell and twisted her ankles, the pain shooting around the bone with knife-thrust sharpness.

Now, when she most needed help, the ford was lonely and deserted; she screamed out the king's name; insanely she screamed his name again and again, but no one heard her; no voice answered. She screamed out the plan to assassinate the king and only a bird squawked out its sudden startlement at the sound of her hoarse voice.

She tried to walk and fell, and tried again, and fell; and then began crawling, and every possible obstacle came to impede her; the skin from her knees was left upon the earth; rough ground and small stones grated away further patches of skin; sand coated the rawness and blood began to drip in warm trickles. The pain in her ankles weakened her and twice she fainted, and each time imagined herself, for a few disoriented seconds, back in the past, escaping with Malanga from his people.

The sky was gathering darkness, the clouds seeming to press down on her. A distance that she could have walked in minutes seemed now to take hours to traverse; the more she strained, the farther away Dukuza appeared.

She mumbled to herself as she crawled; called on Tshaka; was too dazed to think of conserving strength; again and again called on the king and wasted the painful breath she managed to draw into her aching lungs.

'Let me get to you,' she pleaded, as if speaking to the king, snatching at a handful of grass and pulling herself forward, 'let me get to you. They are planning to kill you. I could have warned you. I set myself up as God. I kept the power – of life and death – in my hands. I am not God,' she called wildly. 'I cannot shape a man's destiny,' and for some while she lay prone, exhausted; and then slowly jerked her legs up and looked at her ankles and they were monstrously swollen.

Already it might be too late; like the strangers, she had delayed too long.

The massed clouds above her increased the gloom; and it seemed to her that she was imprisoned in a furnace; that she was being burned up in a mounting fever. Her entire body was wet and little sticks of grass adhered to her; loose sand clung to her and dust streaked her face.

She wiped away some of the dust which had settled around her eyes and which was obscuring her vision, and she thought of Tshaka at the head of his army; and she remembered the cloud of dust which always hung over the army; and she remembered how this dust cloud dimmed the sun.

When at last she came to Dukuza she did not enter by the great entrance but crawled painfully around to the small, secret opening which the women used; dully she realised that if she were seen in her present state questions would be asked and wrong conclusions drawn and she might be kept from the king by force. Perhaps many were conspiring with the traitors; she did not know.

A strange quietness lay upon the area surrounding the royal quarters; was the king dead? Had the people fled at his death? And yet this she did not believe. Somehow his moment of death would be known to her. Might it not be that he had discovered the plot? That his people had hastened away in terror?

So numb she was, so weary, her mind so clouded; with great effort she crawled into her hut and cleaned her face and put on a little bead apron; for the one she had worn, after contact with rough ground and stones, scarcely provided any covering. In the eerie silence even her breathing was too loud.

She tried to hurry but her limbs would not obey her; tried to stand and the pain in her ankles brought her to her knees. She could not crawl into Tshaka's presence; wherever he was, wherever the people were, she could not crawl on her belly like a snake. She took a stick, the stirring-of-the-cooking-pot-stick, and used it as a lever and found that she could just hobble with its aid; the walls of the hut wavered and receded and she closed her eyes and drew upon her waning strength.

She was not conscious of the length of time it took for her to stumble to Tshaka's Royal hut, which she found deserted; at the entrance she stood irresolute, not knowing whither now. It seemed as if he had been spirited away; as if he and his people had vanished without a trace. His sleeping mat lay on the floor, the covering skins warm and thick; various pots were in their usual places; but not here, indeed nowhere, did anything stir. Except perhaps a dog: a sly, shadowy shape crossed from one hut to another, a little distance away.

Then she saw an old man, a very old man, sitting near a hut, his blind face turned towards her; even in age his posture was proud; and he held his head, honourably ringed, as if he were a man of importance.

Slowly, so slowly, she hobbled towards him; he heard her and waited. When she was within speaking distance, she said softly, stilling the urgent desire to scream, 'Father.'

He made no answer and fear gripped her that she was lost in a monstrous dream out of which she would never awaken. The sightless eyes were unaware of her presence; the old ears did not seem to hear. Perhaps she was in the presence of a ghost; perhaps she was in the land of the spirits; perhaps death had claimed her and she had not recognised the lineaments of death.

'Father,' she said again, whispering, her mouth so dry that she could not swallow.

But now the old man made a murmured assent; he was indeed very old; strange it was that he had not been helped home to the land of the spirits in the way of the people when life became a burden because of extreme age.

And then she remembered a man – she remembered a man whom Tshaka had used – a man whose eyes had been removed at the order of the king – a man who had committed some misdeed – a misdeed the like of which Tshaka wished his people to avoid. She looked closer and saw that the man was not so old, but blindness had robbed him of his will to live.

Ah, not now, her heart cried; let nothing now remind me of Tshaka's cruelty; let me remember that what he did, he did for a purpose. But she was sickened.

'Father,' she said respectfully, 'where is the Black One? Where are the people?'

'The Great Elephant has gone to the kraal of the Ugly Year,' the man replied, his voice dull and expressionless. 'Some of the people have gone with him. I heard that men had arrived from far away and that the

Great Elephant wished to receive them at the Ugly Year. And many people have gone to a marriage feast across the hills. Is the sun setting, young woman? Is the sun setting yet?'

'Not yet, my father. There is a darkness because the heavens are black with storm clouds.'

'I cannot see the heavens,' the man muttered and he passed a trembling hand over his blind eyes.

'Father,' Thola whispered, 'I feel that you have lost the will to live. Therefore you have nothing to fear. Therefore you are not afraid. Tell me, Blind One, do you hate the king for what he did to you? Do you wish him blind too?'

As her words died away the intense silence returned; such silence, such a deep, heavy silence.

'I do not hate the king,' the man answered at last, his voice a thread, a small, sighing murmur. 'I would die for the king. I hate my blindness which keeps me from slaying his enemies.'

'He took your eyes from you!'

'Not heedlessly,' the man said, shaking his head. 'I broke the law. I knew I was breaking the law. So it is that I am the cause of my blindness. I blinded myself.'

'The king's guards did that. The king's guards. I remember. I saw them do that terrible thing to you.'

'You are a woman,' the man said proudly. 'You do not understand,' and he turned away from Thola.

'Time is going and soon it will be too late. I must hurry. Old Man! There is something I *must* know. Answer me truly. If Tshaka Zulu – yes, I use that name – if he were in danger of death and you could save him – would you spare his life?'

'I would spare his life,' the man said simply, and kept his face averted.

Thola sighed and moved away and hobbled slowly towards the kraal of the Ugly Year. And now UmuSa was with her, and UmuSa's baby; and regiments of faceless men and women, and children, and small laughing boys; the very young and the very old; and all those who had died in battle; and Malanga, vain and boasting of his prowess; but upon Malanga the greyness of death had not yet fallen; with Malanga marched others, in the bloom of life; but Malanga and his companions were striding on towards a place where corpses lay thick upon the ground; over this place vultures wheeled; to this place obscene animals came at nightfall.

Now she could see the kraal of the Ugly Year and the people grouped there, not many people. And she could see Tshaka seated; the strangers were talking to him, and she could see Umbopha and Dingane and Mhlangana.

If, at this moment, she screamed, she would only precipitate matters; the people would turn their faces in her direction; Tshaka would bend his gaze upon her and his brothers would strike. Umbopha would strike. Such a diversion would meet their needs. If she screamed now she would be aiding the king's enemies.

She attempted to speed up her hobbling pace and her stick struck a stone and twisted sharply and she found herself on her knees, her body jarred in its sudden impact with the hard earth.

While she scrabbled for the stick she heard Tshaka's voice, but distance robbed that deep bass voice of its sonorous rumble. Once again on her feet, she proceeded carefully, cautiously, afraid to waste precious minutes in another fall, distrustful now of haste.

And, as if through a haze, as if through a shrouding mist, she saw Dingane and Mhlangana steal, so secretly, behind the place where Tshaka Zulu sat; and she knew that they were waiting for a signal from Umbopha.

Now she dared not scream; almost she was afraid

that the king would notice her stumbling approach and be distracted; the king needed to have his every thought focused upon himself; he needed every reserve of strength.

Again, far away, somewhere upon the grey sea, lightning flashed through the leaden heavens; a little delay and thunder grated unpleasantly on her ears, muted but menacing.

She entered into the place of the Ugly Year. No one noticed her. No one looked at her. All eyes were intent on the king. If she spoke to the men nearest her they could rush forward and disarm Dingane and Mhlangana; but no commoner would touch the brothers of the king; no man would dare to lay hands upon the person of Umbopha. Would any believe her?

The men from the distant tribe sat respectfully in Tshaka's presence. The wind blew about the king's great shoulders and troubled the oxtail-garland around his neck.

Suddenly, from behind parting clouds, the sun shone upon the king's face; deep shadows formed beneath the heavy ridges of his cheekbones.

The king spoke a few words; his strong bass voice fell upon the people's ears. The people applauded him.

Overhead the clouds massed together again and shut out the light.

18

A BIRD of ill-omen flew overhead and cried plaintively, but Tshaka did not look up. He kept his gaze upon the strangers and his lips smiled gently. His long, beautiful hands were at peace upon his knees, and his breathing was strong and even.

Before many hours had passed the sun would set; now the people gazed at their king as if he were the sun; they saw the magnificence of his physical form but the brilliance of his mind escaped them. They saw in him their bridge between heaven and earth; between their land and the land of the spirits. They saw in him law inviolable and supreme authority.

'Bayete InKosi,' his people saluted him. 'Hail, O Chief!'

If there were those among them who knew that Dingane and Mhlangana skulked behind the place where the king sat, this knowledge they did not reveal.

'Bayete!' the people shouted. 'Bayete!', and the king continued to smile gently.

A shaft of sunlight pierced the gloom again and Thola recalled the day she had first seen Tshaka; as now, that day the sun had placed a patina of gold upon him; as now, he had been splendid and regal before his people. And she recalled many other things: his inhuman control, his steadfastness of purpose, his unexpected gentleness and kindness.

Umbopha moved restlessly, but this was not yet the signal, and Tshaka Zulu lived on; but the darkness of death was gathering around him.

Thola recognised the man who had spoken to her at the river-ford; he was explaining to the king that heavy rains had delayed his passage and that of his companions. But he had much to show the king, articles which he hoped the king would find pleasing.

'You saw perhaps the white man, Fynn, who is my friend?' Tshaka asked, his mock anger at the strangers' delay replaced by good humour.

'That we did not, Great One,' the stranger replied. 'We wished to reach the Great Elephant as speedily as possible.'

Now a weakness invaded Thola and a constriction caught at her throat. A few steps nearer, she thought. Only a few steps.

'I am awaiting men from Fynn,' the king said. 'They also delay. You will serve my purpose. You will go for me to Fynn.'

That meant, Thola knew, that this was the last she would see of the king; at daybreak she would leave with the strangers and journey with them away from the land of the AmaZulu to Fynn's settlement. She paused, rested upon the stick; her heart beat desperately; she opened her mouth to call the king.

Umbopha gave a sign. Fynn was to record in his diary how Umbopha 'threw a stick' at the men from the distant tribe. Immediately there was confusion, and no one saw a woman fall; no one saw a woman attempting to crawl towards the king. The strangers jumped to their feet and ran, and Tshaka turned impatiently to Umbopha.

At that moment Mhlangana stabbed the king; in his

cowardice Mhlangana stabbed from behind; and the crawling woman screamed too late.

Tshaka Zulu looked around and his eyes rested upon the faces of Dingane and Mhlangana, his half-brothers; his strong voice called, 'What is this, children of my father?'

Dingane stabbed the king; and also Umbopha. Tshaka, in one powerful movement, withdrew the spear from his flesh and the red blood flowed like a river. Already he was dying but he strode forward as if possessed of all his strength; and he towered above all other men; and in his deep voice he prophesied, saying: 'Now will those from across the great water take my country and my people.' He threw his cloak from him and his deep wounds were revealed. He did not sink to his knees; as a great pillar crashes down, so was Tshaka Zulu brought low by death.

He prophesied truly and his people ever remember his words.

The breath of life departed from him. Sigidi, Sidlodlo Sekhanda, he who was the equal of a thousand, he who was the pride and the honour of the regiments, was no more.

Two of his chiefs, running to his side, were killed; his people fled and cowered far from his kraals; but at last they gathered together and sang and made 'funny faces', that is, sadness disfigured their features and the tears streamed down their cheeks, and their voices were small because of the sorrow in their hearts.

Above the driving wind a woman called, 'Hamba gahle. Go well.'

No voice answered her; no deep bass voice said, 'Sala gahle. Stay well.'

No man dared touch the body that had held the living spirit of Tshaka Zulu. The king lay spread upon the ground, and the tears of heaven fell upon him and washed away the red blood.

The sun went from the sky and the storm broke and lashed the earth and darkness lay upon the land of the AmaZulu.

Lightning revealed that death had not changed the features of the king.

The people moaned and again fled and the kraal was deserted.

Men went forth to hunt the strangers, for the accusation of murder had been placed upon them by the lying tongues of the traitors.

All through the dark night Tshaka Zulu was left; in the morning preparations were made for his burial. He was gagged so that he would not speak from the land of the spirits; so that his voice would be stilled forever. He was bound in skins and placed in a grain pit, and covered over; and warriors came to stand guard at his grave.

Throughout his kingdom the people were desolate.

Dingane and Mhlangana attacked Ngwadi, the son of Nandi, the half-brother of Tshaka Zulu; that brother who had been loved by Tshaka Zulu. Many attacked Ngwadi; and Ngwadi and his followers were few against so great a number. Before Ngwadi died he killed eight men; he and his men fought to the last, to the very last; they took with them into the land of the spirits hundreds from the ranks of the attackers.

Mhlangana, he who had stabbed first, did not benefit by the going of Tshaka Zulu; within two months he too was sent into the land of the spirits.

Dingane became the ruler of the AmaZulu; slowly, cunningly he took out of the land of living those great ones who had loved Tshaka Zulu; he encouraged the lying tongues of devious men; he put the name of Tshaka Zulu in disrepute. But Dingane was not loved; he was not revered. He could not hold his people together; he could not induce a nation of many tribes to remain a unit. He was treacherous and cruel for cruelty's sake.

And the people came to fear Tshaka as if he were indeed a living force; they would not speak of him; they believed that he roamed the hills and the valleys at night with his spirit impis. They said: 'He foretold much and what he foretold came true.' His name they did not use.

In the darkness of night they cowered and said, 'Listen!'

And all would listen; in the silence they would listen and tremble.

'He watches,' the people said. '*He* waits.'

And always the winds echoed that great, hissing war cry: 'Si-gi-di!'